'You brat!'

Paul whirled r[...]
but an ill-br[...]
unseasoned. Green right through to the heart.'

Reduced to a terrified silence, Taffy dared a glance at him. 'Just because I let you kiss me...'

'You shouldn't start what you don't intend to finish.' His voice came from deep in his throat, each word as sharp as a bullet. 'Did nobody ever tell you that?'

Dear Reader

Do you enjoy travelling to new and exciting places? Well, look no further every month than your favourite Mills & Boon romances, which are offering you the chance to see Europe, and to relax with a top-flight love story at the same time! This month, in our series of stories which we've chosen for you to celebrate 1992—a special year of European unity—you'll find yourself transported to the delightful country of Luxembourg, which is known as 'the green heart of Europe'. So, as they say in Luxembourg, *En voiture*, or *Instappen* (all aboard)!

The Editor

The author says:

'"You'll love it," a friend said, when I was first to visit Luxembourg. "Such pretty hats"! They were, and I did. I was a young wife then, and this dream city is the perfect place to be young and in love. Since then, I have visited Luxembourg, "island" and city, many times. I was never able to stay as long as I wanted: there wasn't time. I can't tell you here about all the reasons why I love Luxembourg: there isn't space. But some of them I have put into my story. For the rest, well, why not go and find out for yourself?'

Jessica Marchant

*TURN TO THE BACK PAGES OF THIS BOOK FOR **WELCOME TO EUROPE**... OUR FASCINATING FACT-FILE*

THE
GREEN HEART

BY
JESSICA MARCHANT

MILLS & BOON LIMITED
ETON HOUSE   18-24 PARADISE ROAD
RICHMOND   SURREY   TW9 1SR

First published in Great Britain 1992
by Mills & Boon Limited

© Jessica Marchant 1992

Australian copyright 1992
Philippine copyright 1992
This edition 1992

ISBN 0 263 77755 3

Set in Times Roman 10 on 11½ pt.
01-9210-52571 C

Made and printed in Great Britain

European Community

1	EIRE	4	NETHERLANDS	7	GERMANY	10	FRANCE
2	U.K.	5	BELGIUM	8	PORTUGAL	11	ITALY
3	DENMARK	6	LUXEMBOURG	9	SPAIN	12	GREECE

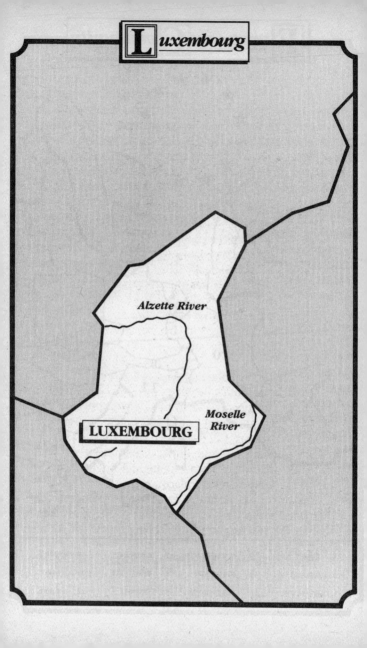

CHAPTER ONE

'MONSIEUR...' Taffy squinted once more at the name by the doorbell. 'Monsieur Seyler?'

'Paul Seyler.' Hand on the door he had just opened, the tall stranger bowed his smooth, dark head in formal greeting. 'And you——' his deep tones easily rode the party babble from the rooms within '—are Miss Davina Griffin, from the flat below.'

Taffy was taken aback. 'How did you know?'

Now why on earth was she shivering, on this August evening? It wasn't any big deal his knowing her name; she'd printed it and put it by her own doorbell three days ago, when she'd moved in. Yet here she was, trembling in the soft breeze that played on her through the open window.

'You're the neighbour my nephew hasn't managed to see yet,' he explained bewilderingly. 'Though he assures me he's been trying all afternoon,' the deep voice added with its lilting accent. 'I even telephoned you myself, a couple of times.'

'I was doing the tour of the Casemates,' she found herself explaining. 'Then I thought I might as well go on to the Grand-Ducal Palace...'

She broke off, annoyed at her own apologetic tone. She wasn't here to give an account of her movements, nor to ask his forgiveness for being out when he tried to reach her.

'That's a lot of sightseeing for one Saturday,' he commented with a brief half-smile. 'I would guess you are newly arrived in our city, Miss Griffin?'

7

'I've been here a whole week... So you're a Luxembourger?' she asked, diverted once more in spite of all her efforts.

'There are some of us about——' again that smooth, formal bow, but with ironic overtones '—here in Luxembourg.'

'Not so many as all that,' she flashed, stung. 'With all the different nationalities working in this city, I've hardly met any Luxembourgers yet, not socially...'

She broke off to glance down at her knee-length robe, its moss-green folds dancing in the breeze from the window. You could hardly call this a social meeting. She'd better get back to her reason for being here, and not let him distract her further.

'I've come up about the row you're making...'

Oh, dear, she hadn't meant to be as aggressive as that. It was only those maddening party noises, filtering through her ceiling for the last two hours, which had made her own loneliness seem a hundred times worse.

The warmth had faded from the craggy features like sunlight from a rocky landscape. 'That——' his voice had dropped, and he bit every word off, clear and careful '—is why I told my nephew to see you. To warn you——'

'Warn me!' Her temper fizzed up again. 'So it's all right to be rowdy, as long as you give advance warning?'

'And to say,' he continued, smoothly determined not to be interrupted, 'that it would all be over at ten.'

'Oh. Well...' She looked down at her high-heeled mules, feeling foolish. 'It didn't sound like it.'

His arched brows drew together over the jutting nose. 'Do you usually guess how long a noise will last by the sound it makes?'

'You know what I mean,' she snapped, maddened by her own absurdity. 'That kind of music generally goes on all night.'

'And speaking of sounds——' he nodded down to where her thumb still rested on the bell, her fist closed tight round her precious front-door key '—did you need to press that quite so hard?'

'I had to be sure you heard.' But she snatched her hand to her side, the key digging into her palm. 'The noise you're making in there——'

'Really, *mademoiselle*,' he cut in impatiently, 'it is not so bad even up here. And I know that the sound-proofing in these flats is good.'

'I happen to be trying to sleep right under...'

She trailed off, biting her lip. Now she'd given herself away, the wallflower who stayed in on a Saturday night when everyone else was out enjoying themselves. Not only stayed in, but wished she were back home in Shepton...

No, she didn't. She'd make friends in time, even if all her office colleagues at the European Centre did seem so old and sophisticated. She refused to be homesick, or to miss her family. She just wouldn't.

'Trying to sleep, at twenty past nine?' The infuriating man raised a strong wrist to glance at a perfectly crafted gold watch. 'You can hardly blame us for the early hours you keep.'

'Yes, I can!' Was this really her own voice, so edged and explosive? 'I mean, if a person wants to sleep——'

'Wait.' The deep tones growled through hers like an engine roaring through an escape of steam. 'You need to calm down.'

Didn't she just! What a way to introduce yourself to a new neighbour! And he would just have to be a

Luxembourger, wouldn't he? One of the very people she
most wanted to meet, a local among all the foreigners.

He was also, she reluctantly admitted to herself, quite
right about the noise. It wasn't anything like as loud
down there as she was making out. It only upset her
because she already felt so lost, such a long way from
anybody who cared about her...

I am not homesick, she told herself silently, spelling
it out in her own mind to be quite sure she understood
it.

And who was this man to decide what disturbed her
and what didn't? Another record began, with the woman
vocalist whose style Taffy's father had often called 'ripe
bananas'. The guests raised their own voices to be heard
over it, the clamour swelled, and Taffy felt more lonely
and left out than ever.

'It's all very well for you,' she burst out anew. 'If
you'd been down there in bed with me...'

She trailed off, and fastened her appalled gaze on the
silvery leaf-pattern of his tie. The droop of her head
brought light brown curls bouncing over her face and
she left them there, hoping they would hide the glowing
heat she could feel rising in her cheeks.

And why on earth hadn't she put on some clothes
before rushing up here? It wouldn't have taken her a
minute to scramble into jeans and a T-shirt. But no, she'd
been too impulsive as usual, determined to complain
before she lost her courage. And here came another
shiver at the sound of that deep, mocking voice.

'Do you wish to rephrase that?'

At least he'd spared her the wisecracks. She dared to
look up at him, though she knew her own face would
still be crimson.

'Your party would never have worried me when I was
living at home,' she admitted. 'In Shepton, Saturday used

to be my night for having fun. Not——' she rushed to correct the false impression she might have given '—not fun in bed, I didn't mean...'

Oh, dear. She saw the hard mouth quirk, the dark gaze linger on her flimsy robe, and had to resist the urge to fold her arms protectively round herself. For the life of her, she couldn't help nervously touching the button below the deep V of her neckline.

It was closed, and so no doubt were the others all the way down. She'd bought this négligé for the way its green lit her hazel eyes to the same colour. She could never for a moment have imagined how, here in the white blaze of the staircase light, it would make her feel so...so exposed. She knew, she just knew he could see through the fluttering silk to where her skimpy nightdress ended and the rest of her...went on without it.

'Fun in bed,' he repeated with relish. 'I like it.'

'Most men do,' she blurted out, alert and defensive.

'I only meant I enjoyed your way of putting it,' he explained with devastating calm. 'It's neat, it's short, and it says all that needs saying.'

'It does not! There's a lot more needs saying before you start anything like that.' She forgot all her embarrassment in the heat of this opinion she had expressed so often, to so many male companions. 'Fun in bed doesn't mean a thing, except that a man and a woman——'

'Fit together like foot and shoe?'

'I wouldn't have put it quite like that, but it'll do.' She glanced up, met the calm, enigmatic gaze, and looked quickly away. 'Yes, your shoes need to fit, but they aren't everything. There's a lot of other stuff that has to fit as well...'

She trailed off, and dared another glance at him. How much had she given away of her hopes and dreams? Of the reasons she had always held back from that first, fateful step into womanhood?

Beyond him in the flat, a new record had started. 'Love me for life,' the woman vocalist wailed, 'or don't love me at all.'

Which just about summed it up, thought Taffy, and, what was more, he knew it. She didn't understand quite why she was so sure, but she could see it somehow in the tiny frown, the measuring dark eyes, the hard mouth set to a new briskness.

'Right.' His vigorous tone cut through the lyric. 'Message received. But as one neighbour to another, Davina Griffin——' his glance swept down to her dancing hem, then up to where the green silk rose and fell with her breathing '—if you don't want to be...tried on,' the deep voice lingered on the words, their meaning quite clear, 'you'd be wise not to go about looking so tempting.'

She flung back her head in outrage at the unfairness. 'I wouldn't be going about at all,' she pointed out, 'but for you keeping me awake while I was trying to sleep...'

Oh, dear. She caught the sudden, dangerous gleam beneath the long lashes, and felt a pulse hammer in her throat. This time he wasn't going to let her off so easily.

'I'm really supposed to have done that?'

'You *did*,' she insisted, though her mouth was dry and her breath playing tricks on her. 'Why else would I be up here?'

'I don't know. But I do know this.' The deep voice sank to a velvety purr, and his lips parted for a moment to show the tip of his tongue between white, even teeth. 'If I'd been the one keeping you awake, you'd be a hell of a lot less skittish by now.'

'Skittish!' She jerked her head up, careless of the new rush of heat in her cheeks and the curls bouncing at the nape of her neck. 'What a beastly thing to say!'

'It fits.'

'You make me sound like a mare in heat.'

'Not a mare.' The disquieting dark gaze measured her, up and down, side to side. 'Definitely not a mare.'

'I d-didn't m-mean...'

She stammered to a halt, and tried to brace herself by straightening her shoulders. Too late, she realised how she had thrust out her breasts, and how her ragged breathing made them more prominent still. She could see them, down there at the lower edge of her field of vision, négligé sliding about over nightdress, and, under that, nothing but her.

Well, just let him try staring directly at them. Just let him dare! To take her mind off them, she tried to speak again.

'I don't think——'

'If we're talking animals——' the soft purr cut with ease through her uncertain stammer '—yours is a dormouse.'

She gazed at him in speechless indignation. This was getting worse and worse.

'An *edible* dormouse.' His tongue had crept out again to moisten his full lips.

Full? She stared at them in fascination. Hadn't they been straight, hard, unyielding, when she first saw him? But yes, they did have an inner fullness, visible only at times like this when he chose to show it.

'Edible,' she choked, desperate for distraction. 'That's something you eat. Who'd want to eat a mouse?'

'The Romans used to. A special one with a bushy tail——' his hand stole out and lifted her curls from her neck '—like this.'

She jerked her head away, but his hand had already gone.

Only the lightness of it stayed with her. That lifting and dropping of her hair had started a tingling which seemed to spread inward to her scalp, down the back of her neck where his fingers had never touched, on along her spine and through her body until she couldn't think straight any more.

What had he been talking about? She pressed the toothed edge of her key into her palm, and tried desperately to remember. Yes, that was it, he'd been comparing her with some kind of mouse that people used to eat.

'They liked it fat,' he added.

That did it. 'Fat!' She came abruptly to herself, and pulled in her abdomen until it was positively concave under the whispering moss-green. 'I am not——'

'No. You're not.'

But his glance lingered exactly where she had promised herself she would never let it. And instead of crushing him with a few well-chosen words, instead of turning away and leaving with dignity, all she could do was stare back at him. Stare up into those dark eyes under the curved brows, let them take her and hold her and do what they would with her...

'What's up, Paul?' a male English voiced called from the babble within the flat.

Taffy jumped, and breathed out a sigh of relief. This was more like it. Though she couldn't see this new speaker, something about that voice already made her feel more at home.

'It's nothing,' Paul Seyler, suddenly taller than ever, threw back over his shoulder without moving.

'What's keeping you, then?'

The voice was nearer now, in the hall, almost with them if her companion had allowed it. But he stayed blocking the doorway, not moving except to turn and throw back another putting-off answer.

'We're nearly through.'

'No, we're not,' Taffy contradicted indignantly. 'I haven't had any satisfaction about this noise.' She raised her voice to call round him, 'I'm trying to tell your host——'

'My what?' the other voice broke in. 'You've got it wrong, missy... Dammit, Paul, let a guy through, will you?' A scuffle, a shuffle, and the other man had dodged past the tall figure in the doorway to stand clear before her by the window. '*I'm* the one who's host round here...' His mouth dropped open. 'Blimey!'

His gaze wandered over Taffy with such delight that she felt her composure returning. She never took this kind of admiration seriously, especially not from someone so young and wine-stained and wine-dazed, but she knew now why his voice had cheered her. It was because he was so like her youngest brother. He even looked the same, lanky and gangling and never quite in control, still stumbling his way into manhood.

'You old fox, no wonder you didn't want me in on this.' He spoke to one side, never taking his eyes off Taffy. 'I'm Nick Eliot, gorgeous.'

'And I,' she felt herself relax into her bossy, sisterly manner, 'am in the flat below...'

'That near? How lucky can a guy get?' He breathed it out very softly, as if she were a soap-bubble that might blow away. 'I wasn't even sure you were real.'

'Well, I am.' She knew exactly how to handle this. 'Real, and alive, and kicking about the noise...'

'The music, you mean?' He opened his arms, and swayed in time to the new smoochy record. 'Come on, let's dance.'

'Thank you, no.' She took a step back from him.

'Aah, now, gorgeous——'

'I said no!'

She put an edge of command in her voice. This was exactly the kind of young male with more energy than sense, like her three brothers and their friends, that she had dealt with all her life. She straightened, as formal as it was possible to be in nightdress and robe, and called on the secretarial training which had taught her the importance of names.

'And if this is your party, Mr Eliot——'

'Call me Nick, gorgeous——'

'I think not, Mr Eliot. And *my* name is Davina Griffin, not——' she gave the word heavy and distasteful emphasis '—not *gorgeous.*'

Nick Eliot's head jerked back, as if she had thrown cold water over him. 'All right, all right, Davina,' he muttered, all injured surprise. 'Keep your hair on.'

'Round one to the lady,' Paul Seyler murmured, a smile just beginning in the dark eyes.

Taffy turned on him with dignity. 'This isn't a boxing match, Mr Seyler.'

'I stand corrected, *mademoiselle.*'

She sensed that he was making fun of her, but somehow she didn't mind. In a part of her she wouldn't acknowledge, she was glad to have shown him how cool and competent she could be, when she wasn't thrown by... But never mind what had thrown her. She turned again to the gangly creature she already, in spite of her rebuke, thought of as Nick.

'About this party, Mr Eliot. Do you think you could tune it down a little?'

'Or we could just dance.' With wine-dazed bravado, Nick moved in to grab her waist.

Taffy fixed him with a Medusa glare. When that didn't work, she put her key on the window-sill, to free both hands if she needed them, and spoke very slowly and clearly.

'Take your hands off me.'

'Come on, give a little——'

'She will not.'

The steely interruption cut Nick short. His grip broke and he staggered back, shirt rising round his ears as his collar was seized in a ruthless grip. Paul Seyler, holding him by the scruff like a kitten, gave him a shake.

'Are you going to behave yourself?' He didn't sound all that angry, but he did sound infinitely, alarmingly determined. 'Or do I have to teach you a lesson?'

'Cut it out, Paul!' Nick squirmed sideways in the iron grip. 'I was only——'

'Only being a damn nuisance.'

'She liked it——'

'And how do *you* like this?' with another shake.

'Watch out for this shirt, it cost me an arm and a leg——'

'Do you like being manhandled?' Another shake rucked the treasured shirt ever higher. 'Do you?'

'Of course I don't, you blasted——'

'So now you know. Apologise to the lady.'

Still held by the collar, Nick caught Taffy's eye with hangdog schoolboy guilt. 'I'm sorry, gorgeous——' Another shake rattled him to silence, and he tried again. 'I mean, *Miss Griffin.*'

Taffy nodded, and couldn't help smiling. If these two only knew it, she had been enjoying the way they could tussle and argue without any real ill-will, as much at ease with each other as her own brothers.

'Nick, darling,' the new voice soared feminine and seductive over the party noises, 'what's keeping you?'

'Be right with you, Claudia.' Nick struggled to free himself, his whole body pointing back to the party like a hunting dog. 'Lay off, Paul. I've apologised, haven't I?'

Still indulgent, the bigger man released him, and stood aside to let him return through the doorway. This Claudia must be quite a woman, Taffy thought, to command such instant obedience. Well, almost instant. Nick was pausing in the doorway for a final stare at the moss-green silk blowing around her own curves.

'Why don't you come to my party, gor——?'

Paul Seyler took a threatening step towards him.

'Miss Griffin,' Nick amended hastily, and added with a beaming, fuddled smile, 'At least you'll let me call you Davina?'

'You can call me Taffy,' she told him, glad to be generous in her new sense of safety.

'Nick!' From within, the Claudia-voice grew exasperated. 'Are you coming in here, or do I send somebody out to get you?'

'I'm there, I'm there. Don't go away, Taffy. Bring her in, Paul.' And Nick vanished into the open doorway.

'At last,' the unseen Claudia reproached him. 'And what's happened to Paul?'

'Some old trout's complaining about the noise.' Nick's careless tones rang back to the landing. 'You know how good he is with old trouts——'

Further revelations were cut off by the door. Paul Seyler had sprung back, and in one lithe movement pulled it almost shut. Taffy blinked across at him, not knowing whether to be annoyed or amused. Dormouse she might be, old trout she definitely was not.

'Is that his wife?'

'Little Nick, with a wife? That'll be the day.' The deep voice changed to a set, cool exactness. 'Do you see now what I mean? What happens when you wander about like that?'

'So it was all my fault, was it?' she demanded, stiffening.

He shrugged. 'These apartment stairs are nearly as public as the street . . .'

'That's got nothing to do with anything. If I walked around here stark naked——' she saw the dark eyes gleam but rushed on with her argument '—that wouldn't be any excuse for any man to carry on the way he just did.'

'Which is why I dealt with him.'

'Thank you for nothing. If you hadn't been making the row in the first place . . .' She broke off, confused. 'I mean, well, I see now it isn't your row, but it's still going on, isn't it?'

'Until ten. If you can bear it for another——' he glanced at his watch '—thirty-five minutes, I promise you it'll stop.'

Oh, dear. Now she felt exactly what Nick had called her, an old trout, in behaviour if not in years. She turned away to the window, glad of the cool breeze on her face, and reminded herself she had every right to object to Nick and his behaviour.

'The very idea that I'd *like* the way he grabbed me!'

'He'll learn. He's only twenty.'

'I'm only twenty-two, but I wouldn't maul any passing man I happened to fancy . . .'

She broke off. The dark eyes had lengthened, lines raying across the temples and high cheekbones while the long mouth pulled together as if to conceal a smile.

'I'm glad I amuse you,' she told him, all dignity once more.

'It's only the idea...'

He stopped speaking, and let the smile break out fully at last. It came at her like the sun from concealing clouds, and made her see things about him she hadn't noticed till now. There was the cleft in his chin, for instance, and the firmness of his jaw, and the generous line of his lips over those white, even, perfect-bite teeth. But it was his eyes which drew her most, told her most, let her know as they met hers with sudden, complete candour, that he really liked her.

'You're not all that well-equipped to maul passing men, are you?' he went on, still with that heart-stopping smile.

'I...I s-suppose not.'

She did see what he meant. At five foot three she'd have a hard time forcing her attentions even on gangly Nick. As for this granite tower of a man, why, he'd only need to fling her over one of those shoulders...

'I wouldn't want to, anyway,' she said quickly.

'Fancy!' He was still laughing at her.

And she still liked it. He wasn't interested in her wretched négligé any more, though it flew around her worse than ever now she was so near the window. No, he was looking straight into her eyes, straight to her essential being, stirring a new part of her which she couldn't define, didn't even want to think about, but which seemed to have been always within her, waiting for him.

'Er—well.' She stretched out a reluctant hand for her key. 'I suppose I'd better get back.'

'I know Nick's asked you to the party,' he told her gently, 'but you wouldn't like it.'

'Wouldn't I?' She remembered Nick's clumsiness, and sighed. 'I suppose not.'

'Not only because of him.' He must have read her thoughts. 'You just wouldn't be very interested in a lot of middle-aged...what would you call them?' His brows drew together for a moment, till he found the right phrase. 'Media show-offs I think is the expression.'

'Media?' Taffy felt her eyes widen. 'You mean television and things? Is there anybody I'd have heard of?'

He shrugged. 'They're mostly from the recording studios. Nick's half-baked way of advancing his possible career in video.'

'Is that what he does?' she asked, intrigued.

This time Paul Seyler laughed outright, head thrown back and white teeth on full display. 'He'd have liked to see how he's impressed you, but in fact he's still a student.'

'I thought he must be,' Taffy snapped. 'And I wasn't a bit impressed really...' She broke off as a new question occurred. 'Where does a student get the money to throw that kind of party?'

'He's not short of money. And, of course, it's my flat.'

'You're letting him use your home, for this party that bores you so much?' She stared up in bewilderment. 'That seems very generous...'

'I suppose it would be, if it were my home.' The dark gaze hooded, veiling its secrets. 'In fact, I'm only here because they asked me if I'd look in.'

'They?' Remembering the confident, commanding tones of the woman who had summoned Nick back to the party, Taffy tossed up her key and caught it, tossed it up and caught it. 'You mean him and that woman he called Claudia?'

He nodded, that gleam of amusement back in his eyes. 'What a lot of questions you ask, Miss Griffin. Yes, Claudia too...'

'Aaah!' It was a wordless squeak of dismay as the wretched key shot away from her and, shining dull-yellow like some exotic insect, spun through the window to vanish into the summer night.

'Shuttlecocks!' Taffy stared at him in dismay, too agitated to notice the mock-swearword of her childhood. 'I'd better get down there...'

'In a minute.' He reached the window in one long stride, and leant over the sill. 'First we'll check where it's gone.'

'Don't be silly, we know where it's gone.' Nevertheless she joined him at the window-sill, to peer with him into the lamp-lit street two floors below. 'It'll be down there on the pavement, and if I don't pick it up quickly——'

'No.' He leant further out, and gestured with a sweep of his powerful forearm. 'Look.'

She followed his pointing finger. Sure enough, there was her key, caught among the stone grapes and vine-leaves of the first-floor balcony's decorated balustrade.

'Oh, dear! Not the grand flat next door to mine?' she exclaimed in dismay. 'I haven't met the people there yet.' She turned to him, reluctantly pleading. 'I suppose you couldn't go with me? Just to ask them...'

'I could,' he agreed easily, 'but not yet. They're away until Monday morning.'

'What? Oh, hen's bellies...'

She trailed off, horrified and helpless. Was she to drift about the staircase like a ghost for the rest of the weekend? A moss-green ghost with far too few clothes on? She looked down at her négligé almost with hatred, and started up in panic as she felt once more that gentle lifting and dropping of her hair.

'It's all right.' He didn't attempt to touch her further, and his voice was low and soothing. 'Stop worrying, dormouse. You'll get in all right.'

'But how? When?' She flung away from him, desperate to shake off the new, distracting rush of her senses to that place at the back of her neck where his fingers had almost brushed her skin. 'I know there are firms you can call when you've locked yourself out, but it's the weekend...'

She broke off with a muffled scream. Vaguely convinced she must at least get back to her own front door, she had made for the stairs, and immediately caught one of her high-heeled mules on the top step. For a seemingly endless moment she staggered, clawed for the banister, missed, and felt herself terrifyingly balanced over nothing, falling, out of control...

'Idiot!'

His voice exploded in her ear, but she was caught, and held, and safe. He must have grabbed the back of her robe with lightning speed; she could feel the buttons straining and popping, something ripping, something flopping down the stairs...

'Damn silly shoes.' Could it have been her slipper he'd kicked out of his way? 'Here——' he was with her now, scooping her off her feet '—you'd better let me get you down there safely.'

'I'm perfectly all right...'

But she wasn't. Her cheek was pressed to his shoulder, her waist supported by one of his arms, her bare knees by the other. Bare because the ripped négligé was already clear of them and riding higher by the second.

And oh, dear, those buttons had gone from the very last place she could spare them. She glanced down to where the robe gaped wide at the top. Beneath it, a little edging of nightdress rose and fell, perched on the outer edges of decency and not likely to stay there much longer. She flung a concealing arm across it, and felt her hand come to rest on a wool lapel. The broad chest beneath it rose and fell like her own, the heart within sending its own muffled message to her fingers.

'Where are you taking me?' she asked, half stupefied.

'Your flat.' His breath stirred her hair with some herbal, elusive fragrance. 'Out of harm's way.'

'But you can't.' She pushed convulsively away from him, then had to flop back as she felt her nightdress slide ever lower. 'We can't get in...'

'We can.' He held her tighter, and continued his smooth progress down the stairs. 'You could have broken your neck. Thank heaven I was there to catch you.'

'But if you hadn't been, I wouldn't have...' She gave up, too weak to argue. 'You can put me down now.'

'In the middle of the staircase?' He kept going. 'You'll stay right where you are, out of trouble.'

'You call this out of trouble?' She grabbed her robe back together. 'I'm homeless, I'll be indecent any minute...'

'But still in one piece. And you're not homeless.'

He reached her front door, and set her on her feet before it with unexpected gentleness. Such gentleness that she had to resist the urge to fling herself back into his arms, and just lie there, and let him take care of her. She turned away, from him and that awful, blank, unenterable front door, and bent down to the torn moss-green silk.

'Buckets of spit, look what you've done to me.'

'I should have just let you fall, I suppose.' He was taking something from an inner pocket. 'What is all this about shuttlecocks, and hen's bellies, and buckets of spit?'

'What? Oh.' She gave up trying to piece the silk together. 'Was I really saying those things?'

'With feeling.'

'I used to invent them to annoy the grown-ups.'

It all seemed a long way off, and yet good to think about. She suddenly found herself much more relaxed, even able to smile into the dark eyes so intent above her own.

'And did it?' His voice had a new throatiness.

'Annoy them? Only in fun. Ma used to say she'd wash my mouth out with soap.'

'Soap, eh?' His gaze dropped to her mouth and lingered there. 'That's not what I'd do with it.'

Taffy suddenly felt as if she were breathing in tension from the very air. Her blood leapt, her scalp tingled, her knees threatened to give way like the joints of an unstrung puppet. The cool edge of the door-jamb bit into her palm as she clutched it tight, bracing herself.

'And what...?' She could hardly get it out, her tongue felt so stiff and heavy. 'Wh-what would *you* do with it?'

'Don't, little Taffy.' He turned away from her. 'Don't tempt me, or I might not be able to stop.'

'I see what you mean.' She gathered her rags together, and glanced around the bright landing. 'Somebody might pass any minute.'

'If I start kissing you while you're like that——' he busied himself with whatever it was he had taken from his pocket '—I wouldn't notice a herd of stampeding elephants. But I don't suppose——' he flourished the small metal object on its jewelled chain '—that you keep many elephants in here, do you?'

And while she looked on round-eyed, he opened the door of her flat and swung it inwards for her.

CHAPTER TWO

TAFFY limped through the open doorway because it seemed the only thing to do. One foot bare, the other trailing its high-heeled mule, she fumbled for the not yet familiar light-switch. It clicked on, and in the muted yellow radiance of her own hall she slung the single slipper off the end of her foot, away into her pink-lit bedroom. What, she wondered, had happened to its partner, which Paul had kicked down the stairs?

He had come in after her, and pushed the door to. She saw he hadn't closed it, and didn't know whether to be glad or sorry. She didn't know what to feel about anything any more, relief at being inside warring with fear that he, a stranger, could have come in here any time he wanted to. Her home was unsafe.

'You've...' She swallowed, clutched her tattered robe about her, and tried again. 'You've got my key.'

'It's yours now.' He showed it on one big palm, a faceted gold chain with a pink coral heart at one end, the key at the other. 'Here.' He deftly detached the chain, and offered the key alone.

She stared at the naked thing, not wanting to touch it. 'How do I know it's the only one around?'

'I believe it is, but——' he dangled the glittering chain, the lonely pink heart swinging to and fro at his will '—I suppose only Annette could tell us.'

'I'd better have the locks changed straight away...' She trailed off. 'Annette Warren?'

He nodded. 'You know her?'

'I took over her job as bilingual secretary.' Taffy sighed at the memory of the elegant blonde who had made her feel such a raw newcomer. 'And seeing she was leaving to be married, I took her tenancy here as well.' She gestured round at the striped wallpaper, the gilt coat-hooks, the long mirror in its gilt frame. 'It's just a nice walk from the European Centre.'

'I know.'

'Yes.' She let her gaze return to the naked key. 'Why didn't you give her it back?'

'I . . . I tried.' He twirled the delicate chain round one finger, uncomfortable for the first time since she'd met him. 'She wouldn't see me.'

'H-had you quarrelled?' Her voice shook.

'You could say that.'

'So she went away——' Taffy felt her strength flowing back in a growing indignation '—having sub-let to me a place where a perfect stranger could walk in any time he wanted to!'

'It's not quite that bad,' the perfect stranger pointed out mildly. 'Technically, I have access to it anyway.'

She stared at him in bewilderment. 'What on earth do you mean? It's my flat, I pay the rent——'

'To me.'

'No, I don't, I pay it to——' she paused to give due weight to the names she had memorised with such care '—to Hansen, Simon et Compagnie.'

'The Hansen retired years ago, the Simon's a cousin of mine, the Compagnie,' with one of his brief, formal bows, 'is me.'

'But th-that means,' she quavered, remembering how rudely she'd attacked him, 'you're my landlord.'

'Something like that. I bought the building years ago, when I lived here myself.' His brisk, dismissive tone made buying an apartment house sound like a very minor detail in his life. 'And I keep that flat on the top floor because it can be useful.'

'Like for giving parties?'

'Like for boosting my wet-behind-the-ears nephew,' with impatient affection, 'in that artistic career he's so keen on.'

'N-nephew,' she repeated. 'Is that Nick? But he's called...' She tried to remember the surname, and got it at last. 'He's called Eliot. An *English* name.'

'It's not allowed?' He proffered the key once more. 'Will you have this, or shall I keep it?'

'I'll take it, I'll take it.'

Forgetting the two edges of silk she had been clutching, she grabbed the key from him. He stiffened, stared down at her, and turned abruptly away.

'Go and change, Taffy.'

She followed his gaze down to her ruined négligé and uttered a small squeak of horror. One of her breasts, flagrantly pink-tipped, was on full display between sliding cotton and torn silk. She jerked her hand back to cover it, so fast that the key dug into her flesh with a chill which would have been welcome if only it had stayed there. But no, it slid from her grasp, down through her rags to her knees, and flopped to the carpet at her feet.

'Oh, dear!' She leaned over to pick it up.

'Leave it!'

He fired the order over her head, hoarsely, with almost desperate urgency. She shot upright, holding the torn skirt of her négligé together with one hand and the buttonless bodice with the other.

'Listen to me, Davina Griffin.' He was still firing, though at some point above her shoulder rather than at her. 'There are three things I could do at this moment. One is to leave...'

'Is . . . is that what you want?' She struggled to hide her disappointment.

'Another is to wait here while you——' his glance flicked over her, and quickly away '—while you cover that glorious body. I can just about manage that, if you hurry.'

'And the third?' It felt like playing on the edge of a volcano, but she had to know.

'The third is to take you in there myself——' he jerked his head at the soft-lit bedroom '—tear off the rest of that stuff you're nearly wearing, and——' he paused, breathing unevenly through flaring nostrils '—and make the most of you.'

'I'm going!' She skipped hastily into the bedroom, and peered out from the safer side of its door. 'And then you'll tell me why you've got that key?'

He dropped to one knee and rescued it from the carpet. 'I promise you, she didn't give them out to all and sundry.'

'She gave one to you, though.'

'I'll wait for you in the living-room.' He set off down the corridor, clearly knowing exactly where he was going.

She closed the bedroom door with a strange mixture of relief and reluctance. The over-large double bed, rumpled as she had flung out of it a lifetime ago, seemed curiously empty now. She let her gaze wander over the thrown-back chaos of the duvet, the serene pink and gold of the bedside lamp, the white of the built-in furniture, the shadowy beige of the carpet. Could this really be the same room she had trailed into at nine o'clock having washed her hair, written home, dusted round, done all the things you did if you'd nowhere to go on a Saturday night?

What a lot had happened to her since then. From the mirrored door of the wardrobe her reflection stared back at her, bedraggled and disquieted, bright-eyed and bushy-tailed . . .

'I am not a dormouse,' she told it, turning away. 'And he needn't think he can eat me, either.'

The novel she had been trying to read lay face down where she had left it. The gracefully entwined lovers on its cover seemed light years away from her now, and yet still too close for comfort. With a quick movement she thrust the book into the bedside-table drawer, then went to put on her briefs and bra.

That was better. Now for her jeans, and what about this new coral-pink T-shirt? She shook it from its folds, held it up, and frowned. In the softness of the lamp the pink cotton glowed back at her, the exact same colour as that abandoned coral heart . . .

She dropped shirt and jeans in a heap, and went instead to her rail of dresses. This one would do, green like the négligé but mixed this time with moth-grey and smoke-blue. She settled the full sleeves round her wrists, widened the drawstring neck to show off her tanned shoulders, and on second thoughts added a lace petticoat under the full skirt. And she'd better wear these slip-on shoes, their flat heels would make her feel safer . . .

Safer? With that man in her home, and her heart doing aerobics whenever he came near her? He stood up when she entered the living-room, and, with one of those formal bows held something out to her. It was the missing slipper, offered with such courtliness that it might have been on a silk cushion, and she Cinderella about to try it on.

'I went out and fetched it as soon as I remembered,' was his far from fairy-tale response to her question. 'We don't want anyone else tripping over it.'

'N-no.' She accepted it a little helplessly, and set it on the coffee-table. 'That's all the bits accounted for, then.'

'Not quite.' And he carefully placed one green button on the coffee-table next to the slipper.

'I lost two...' She lowered her lashes, aware of the heat mounting once more in her cheeks.

He didn't answer. When she next dared steal a glance at him, he had thrust both hands in his pockets and leant forward, closely examining the leaf-patterned carpet.

Which was silly—she hadn't lost the buttons there. She was about to say so when his gaze reached her green shoes and travelled slowly upwards, over each part of her in turn. And oh, dear, here she was shivering again, as if those enigmatic eyes were taking physical possession of her flesh...

'That's... a very nice dress.' His voice broke the spell, though he spoke too loud and too fast. 'You like green, don't you?'

'It's my colour.' She patted the drawstring top with awkward fingers.

It was all right, everything was in place there. She saw with irritation that he was gesturing her to sit, for all the world as if he, and not she, were the host. And he'd lit the china-swan lamp, she noticed, staring into the swirly water patterns of its shade and trying to get herself together.

She'd thought this quite a big room, but he made it seem a doll's house with doll's furniture. Only the armchair he'd risen from was the right scale for him, and she felt a sinking in her stomach as she worked out why. He must have spent a lot of time in that chair, and in the huge double bed...

'Sit down, for heaven's sake,' he broke in on her thoughts.

She flopped to the couch, and resentfully watched him settle opposite in the oversized armchair. His smooth jacket fitted the cushioned shell as if by long habit, and his smooth-suited thighs were exactly the right length for the seat. And if she needed more evidence, look how well he was managing to keep his crowded legs clear of the glass coffee-table.

'I wonder Annette didn't take one of the bigger flats——' Taffy heard her own voice with dismay, yet couldn't keep the resentment out of it '—seeing you and she...' She floundered to silence.

'Hm. Yes. That was more or less her idea.' He stared down at the key. 'Until she decided to rush out and collar...' He caught himself back, and sought another way of putting it. 'And *marry* her Monaco businessman.'

'She said it was a whirlwind romance.'

'Whirlwind, certainly.' He drew the gold chain from his pocket, and stared down at the coral heart. 'What the hell am I going to do with this thing?'

'Put it with your other trophies?' For all her attempt at lightness, it came out venomous.

He darted her a penetrating glance, and shoved the bauble back in his pocket. 'I don't collect trophies,' he answered, utterly simple and direct. 'And this key, this chain, this heart, they were meant to...'

He paused, shifted his feet to within a millimetre of the coffee-table, drew them sharply back. 'Damn it, I'll have to spell it out. Annette was trying to collect *me*.'

Taffy nodded, understanding how easily any woman could want to do that. Even she, who had never run after a man in her life, might have tried for this one if she'd known how.

And it wasn't because he was rich, either. Wealth and success were only outer trappings of the power which infused his whole being, tightened the craggy features and kept the hard mouth from showing its inner fullness. What a privilege to be chosen by him, to know the intimacy of that secret, inner tenderness for the rest of your life ... and what a hopeless dream.

'I suppose,' she ventured, hesitant and sad, 'Annette was only one of many?'

'The one you need to know about.' He face closed up, holding her off. 'I never wanted that damn key.'

'But you did want *her*?' Taffy had to know. 'You must have made love to her often?'

'Often enough, I suppose. There are ways a woman can...' He broke off, frowning. 'But chains, keys, hearts, no.'

'Isn't that a bit mean?'

'No, it damn well isn't!' he rapped, stung to defence. 'You've met Annette, you must have some idea of how she...' He might have been about to say something rude, but stopped in time. 'How she can look after herself.'

Taffy checked her own brief memories. There'd been the hand-over period at work, and the negotiation of terms for the flat. Yes, when you came to think of it, Annette had got the better of those dealings in several ways.

'She made me take this place from the beginning of the week,' Taffy admitted, 'even though she was in it herself for the first three days.'

He nodded, interested but not surprised. 'And she was marrying a man who owned houses in Monaco and Paris, flats in London and New York...'

'A yacht, racehorses, an account at Cartier's,' Taffy continued the recital. 'She did rather go on about it.'

'I bet. But I only heard it once.' The dark eyes met hers with sombre honesty. 'During our last row. Her last attempt——' he shifted in the oversized armchair '—to get *me* to marry her.'

Taffy stored up the warning in a heart grown suddenly leaden. 'I suppose you're just . . . just not the marrying kind?'

'I'm certainly not the being-married-for-my-money kind. And that,' he went on, clearly relieved to be done with the subject, 'is enough about me. Now——' he settled down, in charge without even thinking about it '—tell me about *you*.'

'There isn't much to tell . . .'

But there was. She talked of the pub her parents ran in Shepton, the apple-orchard, the paddock with the ponies who missed her but still had each other. About her brothers, the oldest working in Strasbourg, the next in the navy . . .

'I wonder if they ever get homesick?' she interrupted herself to ask.

'Homesick?' The arched eyebrows rose, the dark eyes lit with a new understanding. 'So that's what it was all about, that attack on my doorbell?'

'No, it wasn't!' The denial came all the quicker for the number of times she had argued it out to herself. 'I've no business at all being homesick, when I've landed the job of a lifetime, in an exciting new city . . .'

'And don't know a soul? And maybe——' the enigmatic eyes roamed over her '—are used to being made a fuss of by the men in your life?'

'My brothers? You must be joking,' she jeered, deliberately misunderstanding. 'They never miss a chance of putting me down.'

'I bet their friends are glad enough to pick you up again.'

'I had plenty of dates, I suppose.' She silently reviewed some of them. 'They all seemed such . . . such stick-in-the-muds.'

Though they'd always got terribly angry if she said that, she recalled with a cautious glance at her companion. Would he agree with the ones who'd told her in return that she was spoilt? That she'd had too sheltered a life, everything made too easy by her adoring parents for their only daughter?

'You expect everybody to run after you the way they do,' one rejected suitor had told her. 'Maybe it's time you got out into the world the way you always say you're going to. You might learn something.'

'If I do, it won't be through going to bed with the likes of you,' she'd retorted, and he'd stamped off in the usual huff.

Men were always stamping out of her life in a huff, even men she quite liked. Sometimes, after the usual quarrel, she would ask herself why she couldn't even keep them as friends. Other girls seemed to.

'My third brother's younger than me. Nearer the age of your Nick,' she added, glad to move on to something more cheerful. 'Are you going to explain now why you have an English nephew?'

'It's no secret. My sister married an Englishman.'

'I see. Then Nick's a half-Luxembourger?'

'For our sins,' he answered with a tolerant grin. 'I got fond of the boy while I was studying in England, ten years ago.'

'So you chose an English university?' She leant forward, fascinated. 'I'd heard how all you Luxembourgers go abroad for your degrees.'

'That's just part of being a Luxembourger. We still . . . well, you know our national motto.' And he went on in his own language, '*Mir wölle bleiwe wat mir sin.*'

'We wish to stay as we are,' she translated, 'and you've done it, right through four hundred years of war and occupation.'

'We go back a lot further than all that. This *Scheuberfouer* Nick's so keen to video, that's six centuries old.'

'The Shepherd's Market?' She thought of vast Glacis Square, which a week ago had blossomed with roundabouts and sideshows. 'It can't always have been a giant funfair, though?'

'It's always been a fair, and they've always had the procession——'

'That's tomorrow, isn't it?' she interrupted eagerly. 'When they decorate the sheep, and lead them round the town with a brass band.'

'Don't they just!' The dark eyes gazed heavenwards in mock endurance. 'Nick's talked of nothing else for weeks. And when Claudia arrived, that did it.'

'Claudia? The lady who called him in?' Who had also demanded to know where Paul was, she remembered with sudden chill. 'Is she another...friend of yours?'

Paul ignored the question. 'As soon as she arrived he asked her to be in the video, if you please, to help sell it.'

'Is she famous, then?'

He shrugged. 'It isn't my kind of thing, but I suppose you might have heard of her.'

The name he mentioned brought Taffy to the edge of her seat. For a moment she couldn't believe it. Then she recalled how the hit numbers filtering down from above earlier in the evening had all featured the same star.

'You've really got Claudia Vaughn, up there at your party?' she breathed. 'Why, she's been at the top of the charts since...' She paused to work it out. 'Since I was about fourteen.'

'Eight years,' he agreed. 'Though it isn't something she likes to be reminded of.'

'But good heavens——' she recalled recent televised glimpses of the slender figure, the mop of blonde hair, the dragonfly clothes '—she only looks about seventeen.'

'Doesn't she, though?' His voice had softened. 'But she's my age, and absolutely hating this thirtieth birthday...' He broke off with another of those closed-up glances, as if a shutter had come down over his thoughts. 'That's really why I let Nick organise this party for her. I hoped it would cheer her up.'

'And put her in the mood for helping with his video?' Taffy asked through the leaden blanket which had suddenly dropped over her. 'It seems a strange idea for a birthday party.'

'Call it more of a birthday tonic. The real party,' and he smiled that brief, sun-warm smile, 'we'll celebrate later.'

She waited for him to say how, but he didn't. She imagined a candle-lit table, attentive waiters, Paul's dark good looks set off perhaps by a dinner-jacket, and sighed. How strange, and how painful, to see the warmth in his eyes, hear the softness in his voice when he spoke of this rich, successful, beautiful woman.

'You're fond of her, aren't you?' she burst out before she could stop herself.

'You could say that.'

It was the exact phrase he had used when talking of Annette Warren, and just as distance-keeping. The hard mouth closed, the dark eyes guarded any show of feeling, keeping her out.

'I suppose I'd better get back,' he added, glancing at his watch.

'Back to Claudia?' She couldn't help it, she had to ask, though she saw with dismay his answering nod.

'She's still jet-lagged. She'll have had enough by now.'

'But didn't you say——?'

'The party would cheer her up? It did,' he confirmed, 'but a little goes a long way. And Claudia seems to tire so easily these days.'

'Is that why it all has to be over by ten?' she asked, talking too quickly to cover her depression.

'That's what Nick promised.' He rose to his feet in a single fluid movement. 'I'd better get up there and see if he's managed it.'

Taffy stayed seated. 'The noise stopped ages ago.'

He cocked a sceptical eye on her. 'I doubt it was ever very loud down here anyway.'

'Loud enough,' she countered. 'If I'd known what it was about, I'd have wanted even more...' She stopped, furious at having given herself away.

Sure enough, he understood exactly. 'You'd have wanted even more to join in,' he finished for her, a half-smile playing about that deceptively straight mouth. 'So you're just another humble fan, little Taffy?'

'Certainly not. I merely thought——' she crossed her ankles, and folded dignified hands in her lap '—that it would be something to write back to my little brother about.'

'How can I resist such a worthy cause?' The smile almost broke through. 'Would you like to come up and meet her?'

'Could I?' She shot from her seat to join him, all dignity forgotten. 'If she's tired, I'll be quiet as a...' She broke off again, newly annoyed with herself.

'As a mouse?' he finished for her with a grin. 'You may have to be, if she's gone to bed.'

'To bed?' Taffy repeated, puzzled. 'In your flat?'

'She stays there whenever she's doing this part of Europe.'

Oh, the easy intimacy in the words! Taffy knew she was round-eyed, but couldn't help it. What a sophisti-

cated world he must live in, where an international star
who was also a close friend would use his flat while
'doing this part of Europe'.

'It's not so very special.' He spoke soothingly, though
the dark eyes had a disturbing gleam. 'It only means
Luxembourg's a bit nearer the middle of things than
you're used to.'

'Shepton isn't the back of beyond,' she began indignantly. 'You can drive to Dover in...' She broke off,
and traced the pattern on the carpet with one green-shod
toe. 'It's true we don't get many pop stars there.'

'So young.' The deep voice lilted with amusement.
'You're right to wear green, little Taffy.'

She flung her head back. 'You make me wish I'd put
on something scarlet.'

'Scarlet.' The dark eyes never left her face, roaming
over her cheeks and forehead and chin. 'With that skin,
that mouth...' His own mouth closed abruptly, and he
straightened. 'Right, so you'll take a chance on Claudia
still being awake?'

Taffy shrugged her bare shoulders. 'What have I to
lose?'

'Hm?' His gaze had dropped to the green dress, rip-
pling and flowing from her shrug. 'Don't worry, we'll
still have Nick about the place.'

Which didn't fit anything either of them had said, but
she somehow knew what he meant.

'He's living there, too?' she asked, as much to break
the tension as to know the answer.

'He has one of the rooms.' Paul gave himself a little
shake, and turned to the door. 'Don't forget your key.'

'I can come in out of the rain, too,' Taffy flared.

'What?' He turned to stare at her in surprise.

'Only that I'm not a complete idiot, even if I...even
if you...' She gave up, took the key from the coffee-

table, and slipped it into her pocket as she followed him into the hall.

'And this time——' he shooed her imperturbably ahead of him '—mind the stairs.'

The upper flat, when he let them into it, was empty and still. The party might never have been, Taffy thought, and struggled to master her disappointment as Nick staggered towards them from the wide-open double doors at the far end of the hall. He came nearer, and she saw that the items he was holding up so proudly for Paul to see consisted of two empty tumblers, a comb, and an enormous pair of sunglasses.

'Found this stuff in there, otherwise the caterers have done a good job clearing up. Hi, gorgeous,' he saluted Taffy, clearly having lost all memory of her name.

'I'll talk to you in the morning,' Paul told him grimly.

'I only had a few glasses of the Riesling.' Nick raised his palm, the comb between two fingers and the sunglasses sliding insecurely to the base of his thumb. 'Scout's honour!'

'A few more than you could handle——'

'You can see I'm fine now,' Nick interrupted, and added with conscious virtue, 'Just doing a final check round, to see I've left everything as I found it.'

'You'd better have. Where's Claudia?'

'Somewhere around.' Nick wove away, clutching his burden. 'The balcony, maybe.'

'Let's see.' Paul beckoned Taffy to follow him through the open double doors.

'Golly,' she exclaimed, unconscious of the childhood slang in her wonder at the room thus revealed. 'Isn't it *huge*?'

'I have all of the top floor.' His casual glance took in the acres of parquet, fringed rugs, marble coffee-tables and enormous leather couches. 'The equivalent of your flat plus what you called——' and he quoted with amusement '—the "grand" one next door.'

'And yet you don't live here?'

'I found somewhere I like better.'

'Even bigger? That alcove——' she nodded to where a full-size grand piano gleamed darkly amid a bewildering array of electronic equipment '—must be about where my entire flat is.'

'I'll check the sound-proofing, if you like.'

He spoke absently, making for the slid-back plate-glass doors in the outer wall. She followed, and found herself out in the summer darkness. Somewhere in the distance the city enjoyed its Saturday night, a car droning, a clock chiming, a plane winking red, green and gold across the sky. Close to, only the lime trees whispered below in the glimmering street-light.

Paul flicked a switch, and a row of wrought-iron lamps glowed to life along the balustrade. They showed a white wrought-iron table, wrought-iron chairs, a striped couch, a striped sun-lounger... Taffy closed her eyes tight and shook her head.

'Turn them off! Please!'

'They bother you?'

He sounded puzzled, but she heard the tiny flick of the switch as he did what she asked. She opened her eyes again with a sigh.

'It's so lovely here without them.'

She moved to the balustrade and drank in the rustling darkness. In the distance, a round tower stood up on the skyline. On the other side of the street, lit windows glowed in the tall black shapes of buildings, and a hundred summer scents lifted to her on the breeze. A smooth movement in the dimness, a shivering warmth at her side, and she knew Paul had joined her.

'This is different from anything at home,' she murmured, just loud enough to be heard. 'I really feel *here* at last.'

'You do?' The teasing lilt was back in the deep voice as he turned to face her, hand out in formal greeting. 'Then welcome to Luxembourg, little Taffy.'

'I'm . . . I'm very glad to be here, Paul.' And she accepted the hand he offered in friendship.

As soon as it touched her own, she knew she had made a mistake. It felt so good, that big, warm, sheltering hand, that she didn't ever want to let it go. She wanted it hers forever, hers to honour and obey, and yet already it was releasing its grip. . . With a small, sinuous movement of her fingers, she stroked their tips against his palm.

It worked like a spark on tinder. He drew a sharp, hissing breath, and caught her to him. She yielded with a sigh to the husky scent of him, of wool suiting and laundered linen and polished leather and clean male flesh, all overlaid with some haunting cologne that reminded her of wild thyme. She knew now that these arms about her, this mouth on hers, were what she'd wanted from the first moment they'd met an hour ago. . .

An hour? It wasn't enough, she must have more time. Time to understand the hard lips which took hers, and opened them, and made her taste the wild-thyme and honey sweetness of his mouth. Time to understand why her tongue should rush so gladly to meet his, why his cupped hand on the back of her head should send such heat down her spine, a brush-fire through undiscovered country. And here was more undiscovered country, here where his other hand pressed her close to his own body. . .

'No!'

This wasn't what she had meant at all. She dragged her lips from his to tell him so, but before she could form the words he had released her. Braced as she had been to fight him, she staggered backwards and had to right herself, cold and alone and washed by a disappointment she refused to admit.

'You shouldn't start what you don't intend to finish.' His voice came from deep in his throat, each word sharp as a bullet. 'Did nobody ever tell you that?'

'I didn't want...I didn't mean...' She broke off, struggling not to be awed by the power she had unleashed. 'Just because I let you kiss me——'

'You didn't let, you invited.' Already the hoarseness of desire was fading from his voice, leaving it tense and controlled. 'After all my warnings.'

'I... For heaven's sake, all I did was...'

'You've used that trick before, haven't you?'

She nodded, not daring to look in his direction even in the soft darkness. 'It wasn't like this.'

Though in fact it had been, a little. The man had been just as angry. Only his anger hadn't counted somehow, any more than his kisses.

She heard a metallic click which must have been the individual switch of the lamp beside them. It lit, and she remembered with a pang how indulgently he had turned all of these lights off when she asked him.

He wasn't about to indulge her any further, that was clear. She stared up to where he loomed over her, and told herself that his anger needn't bother her, it was no worse than any other man's.

'You're nothing but an ill-brought-up little girl,' he snapped, and turned away from her. 'Unripe, unseasoned. Green right through to the heart.'

'Better a green heart than a cast-off coral one,' she retorted to his less frightening back. 'I suppose Annette should have known better than to try and compete with Claudia Vaughn.'

'You...*brat*!' He had whirled round in fury.

Reduced to terrified silence, she dared a glance at him. His eyes flashed in the lamplight like dark crystals, his cheeks had hollowed, his mouth was an indrawn line. A new shiver started deep within her, this time of pure fear.

'Just keep your malicious little mind off Claudia,' he went on, low and dangerous.

She gathered her courage. 'If you feel like that about her, you shouldn't be——'

'*Shut up*!'

She jumped and covered her ears, startled by the sheer volume of his rage. When she tried to face him again, her best efforts brought her no higher than the white of his shirt-front. The silvery leaf-pattern of his tie had the finest overcheck of green, she noticed, like an almost invisible net.

'I will not,' he added, ramming home the message in short, emphatic bursts, 'discuss Claudia with the likes of you.'

'I see.' She tried to swallow down her humiliation. 'And what exactly is the...the likes of me?'

'A frivolous little gossip who'll spread lying rumours about an affair we're not having...'

'How dare you call me a gossip?'

A minute ago, she couldn't have answered him back like that. She was astonished at herself, until her mind caught up with what he'd just said. 'Lying rumours about an affair we're not having' meant that he and Claudia were no more than friends. Somehow her instincts had understood that at once, and responded with a wave of renewed courage.

'In Shepton,' she went on haughtily, 'I am noted for the way I can keep a secret.'

'Oh, yes?' He didn't believe her, but at least he wasn't shouting any more. 'Well, maybe you should have stayed in Shepton, and grown up a——'

'Paul!'

The urgent voice brought them both to attention, facing the plate-glass doors. Nick stood there, wild-haired and wide-eyed, ignoring Taffy and fixing his eyes on Paul as on a lighthouse in a storm.

'Come quick,' he said. 'Claudia's ill. She needs help.'

CHAPTER THREE

'WHERE is she?'

Paul strode in through the window, tensed for action. As the two men faced each other, a part of Taffy's mind noted how they were about the same height, though somehow you wouldn't have thought it.

It's because they're so different, she realised. As if a huge weight's suddenly come crashing down on both, and one can't carry it, but the other can.

Yes, that was it. Nick stood with bowed head, shaken by the crisis, helpless under it, yielding to it. Beside him, Paul was a dark spiral of strength against the brightness of the lamplit room. His polished shoes held the dark gold parquet firm and square, keeping his weight lightly balanced while his hands curved at his side, ready for whatever they had to do.

'Wake up, you young fool.' He grabbed his nephew's shoulders and shook them. 'Where is she?'

'Dining-room,' Nick muttered through chattering teeth. 'She was going to take something to help her sleep...'

Paul flung him aside and vanished, a rushing emptiness where he had been, his feet pounding the corridor out of sight. Nick had staggered and almost collapsed, but managed to straighten up and swivel unsteadily towards Taffy.

'You still here, gorgeous?'

'I...I'd better go, hadn't I?' She moved hesitantly towards him. 'I'm only in the way...'

She trailed off. She'd spoken in good faith, yet the words made her feel like a coward. A runner-away from trouble. A woman deserting a fellow woman in a time of need.

'Do stay.' Nick closed his eyes and shook his head, then gazed at her beseechingly. 'We . . . we may need as much help as we . . .' He slurred to a halt before his own uselessness. 'Another pair of hands . . .'

'I see what you mean,' she agreed, careless of his pride. 'At least I'm sober.' She sped across to him. 'Come on, then.'

'It's that way,' he muttered with a limp gesture. 'I'll get there when I can.'

Really, you could understand Paul's impatience with this lanky, self-indulgent boy. She crossed the great room, out through the double doors, and hurried along the corridor in the direction he had indicated to where the nearest door stood wide.

This must be the dining-room. It was smaller than the other, but still had plenty of space round the long dark oak table and leather-backed chairs. A detached part of her observed half-empty soft-drink bottles on the immense dark oak sideboard, the only sign left of the party. Nick was right about the caterers having done a good job of clearing up—presumably Claudia Vaughn was used to the very best that money could buy.

But money wouldn't buy Paul, Taffy thought incoherently. A strength like his, a tenderness like his, they're not on sale anywhere.

He was gently supporting the slight figure in his arms. He must have just lifted it from that chair which stood skewed out at the end of the table. Spiky shoes lay under the chair, and before it a solitary, unstopped bottle gave out the headiness of high-quality brandy. No, the real source of that was the overturned glass whose spreading contents had soaked the cloth.

'Don't just stand there.' All care, all gentleness for the woman in his arms, Paul didn't glance in Taffy's direction as he nodded at the telephone. 'Call emergency for an ambulance.'

'Emergency?' It was Claudia, weak and sad as a lost kitten. 'Oh, God. What have I done?'

'It's all right, *ma belle*.' He lowered the limp body to the floor, and sank to his knees by it. 'It's going to be all right. You know what to do?' he asked Taffy over his shoulder.

She had already taken the phone from its wall bracket, and nodded without speaking. This was one time she wasn't going to let anything distract her, not even him. With a strong, accurate fingertip she keyed in the number she had so carefully memorised when she first arrived, and, when the operator answered, made her request and gave the address in firm, clear French.

'Well done.' Paul looked at her with new approval. 'The ambulance is on its way, *ma belle*,' he said to Claudia. 'And until it comes, there are two of us here taking care of you.'

Taffy glowed with pride, and waited quietly for her next chance to be useful.

'It isn't me I'm worried about... Aaah!'

Claudia grabbed his hand and held it right, twisting in pain on the deep-pile carpet. Presently the spasm passed and she was still, eyes closed, black and glitter legs splayed from the hem of her exotic indigo and silver dress.

'You should have stayed.' The famous voice was limp and complaining. 'It might not have happened if you'd stayed.'

'You should have looked after yourself.' He stroked the weakly clutching hand. 'How long did you say it's been?'

'Four months.' The bright, blurred mouth hardly moved. 'I meant to see about it after Las Vegas, but then there was this European tour...'

'Find something to cover her,' Paul instructed Taffy. 'The bedrooms are that way.'

She nodded to show she had understood, and hurried back the way she had come along the corridor. The shambling figure of Nick paused questioningly as she passed, but she shook her head and sped on.

This room must be Claudia's, strewn with bright clothes from the wide-open old-fashioned wardrobe. This sunflower-patterned duvet would do. She threw down the red tango skirt and magenta top which lay tumbled over it, hauled it into her arms, and hurried back. Careful not to trip on the trailing corners, she shoved past Nick once more in the corridor. She felt as if she had been away for hours, but in fact she had made it back to the dining-room before him.

'Well done again, Taffy.' The minute he saw her, Paul rose to his feet in one effortless movement. 'I can see I'll be leaving her in safe hands.'

'Don't go! *Please* don't leave me!' The slender figure on the floor convulsed again as Taffy spread the duvet over it.

'The street door will be locked, *ma belle*,' he told her, already in the doorway. 'It's best if I go down and wait for the ambulance.'

'It's all right, sweetie,' Taffy heard herself murmur just as Paul had earlier. 'I'll stay with you.' And she sank to her knees to take the silver-nailed hand in both of hers, stroking and warming it.

'She passed out.' That was Nick, here at last. 'I didn't
know what to do——'

'Out of my way.'

The steely voice brooked no delay. Taffy heard the
scuffle as Nick was thrust aside, but didn't look up.
Something had gone wrong with Claudia's long ash-
blonde hair.

'She's been acting kind of strange ever since you left.'
Nick's voice floated back from the corridor, following
the hurrying Paul. 'I thought it must be jet lag . . .'

'Get yourself some coffee,' the deeper voice ordered
over the sound of the opening front door. 'We may need
you.'

The door banged. Nick didn't come back, so perhaps
he was obeying orders, and getting a coffee.

Taffy gingerly lifted away the ash-blonde wig. Beneath
it, the famous ash-blonde hair clung damp and stringy
to the small head, dewy with perspiration.

'That's better.' Claudia opened the famous tilted dark-
blue eyes, free of pain for the moment. 'Could you do
something about these damn lashes?'

'Sure.' Taffy understood at once, and dropped the wig
to the table in a flutter of silvery strands while she set
herself to the delicate task of stripping away the false
lashes.

'Thanks.' The sparser ones beneath fluttered. 'Is there
a white bit where they've been?'

Taffy admitted it. 'And your lipstick's all over the
place. But don't worry, you're still——'

'Clean me up,' Claudia ordered with a ghostly return
of her commanding manner. 'The stuff's in my bedroom.
Quick!'

Taffy hurried to obey. Returning from her second
journey to the bedroom, she heard the next wordless cry
of pain, and rushed back to take the clenched, clutching

hand. The spasm passed like the others, and the dark blue eyes opened.

'Now, please. If I have to go to hospital,' the words came out slurred under Taffy's carefully applied cold-cream, 'it's good to know I needn't go there painted like a clown.'

'You aren't in the least like a clown.' Taffy wiped off the cream, her towel staining blue-silver, red, and flesh-tint. 'But I agree, you're well rid of this stuff.'

'It weighs you down,' Claudia muttered, deathly tired, 'having to be beautiful.'

'You still are,' Taffy watched the smooth skin streak and pale in the harsh overhead light. 'More so, now.'

'Thanks, kid. I'm glad you were here.'

'Are you?' Taffy controlled her delight, and kept her voice to a sick-room murmur. 'Then so am I.'

'No guy could have done this for me.' The tender mouth sketched a smile. 'Can you imagine Paul acting as a beautician?'

'The mind boggles.' Taffy's answering smile was warm, as warm as the brilliant burst of certainty within her.

She knew now for sure that these two were no more than friends. Something in Claudia's tone when she mentioned Paul, an ease and a lightness, had dismissed the last of her doubts.

The small face turned to one side, relaxing. Without the make-up, it might have belonged to a tired little girl, fallen asleep far from her bed.

'So . . . so defenceless . . .' Taffy murmured to what she thought was the empty room, and jumped to find Nick at her shoulder. He was drinking coffee as ordered, black, from a delicate porcelain cup without a saucer. He didn't bother to offer her any.

'How is she?' He flung himself into the skewed-out chair, carelessly moved the spiky shoes out of the way with his feet, and jumped in dismay. 'What on earth's that?'

Still on her knees, Taffy wriggled round to find him staring at the silky, swirly blondeness by her on the table. 'It's only Claudia's wig.'

'Thank heaven for that.' He flopped back with relief. 'I thought I must be seeing things.'

He took a frantic pull at his coffee, and Taffy returned to her charge. Yes, that was what this poor, frail creature had become, her charge and duty, to be helped in every possible way. She brushed a damp strand from the delicate brow, and noted a pulse in the temple beating through the fine, pale skin.

'I'm here, poppet, just hang on.' And she nursed Claudia through the next spasm of pain.

'Of all times for an ulcer to perforate,' Nick said at the end of it.

'Is that what it is?' Taffy stroked the silver-nailed fingers, relaxed now that the spasm had passed.

'Well, isn't it? My Dad's got one, and he's the same type, rushing about overdoing things...'

'And your father's ulcer perforated?'

'No, but they told him what it would be like if it did.'

'Then you should have had a better idea of what to do,' Taffy said sharply.

'And the Shepherd's March tomorrow...' The rebuke washed off Nick without a trace. 'Wait a minute.' He stared at Taffy. 'It'll all be in long shot. The sheep, the shepherds, the pretty girl on the roundabout...'

'What are you on about now?'

He shaped his hands into a television screen and regarded Taffy through them. 'Would you mind trying that wig on?'

'What?' She stared back in disbelief.

'You're a different build, but from a distance...'

'For heaven's sake, Nick! At a time like...'

She broke off and strained forward, listening. Sure enough the lift had come to rest on this floor. She could hear its doors opening, then the small grating noise of a key in the front door. As Paul had promised, it had only been a few minutes.

The next events passed in a blur. First came the stretcher men, quiet and kind, murmuring to Paul in their own language, covering Claudia with their own blanket for the journey to the hospital. Taffy knew it was the right thing, the only thing, yet felt almost saddened that there was no more she herself could do to help. When Paul opened the front door and the stretcher silently disappeared, it left a blankness in her.

'So what now?' Nick asked, hovering like Taffy on the edge of the action.

'For you, sleep.' Paul had returned from the still open front door. 'We're going to the hospital, to wait.'

'We?' Taffy looked down at his outstretched, guiding arm. 'You want me to come, too?'

'I watched you while they were taking her away,' he said as if that meant yes. 'You care what happens to her, don't you?'

'She's nice,' Taffy confirmed, hushed with her sense of awe and privilege. 'I want her to get well.'

'You get attached to people when you've looked after them.' He re-opened the front door and gestured her through it. 'Go to bed,' he told Nick, who had drifted out after them and now hovered just inside the door.

'But I... But you...'

'Goodnight.'

And Paul quietly but firmly closed the door. Taffy half expected Nick to open it again, as she would have herself, but he didn't. It stayed shut all through her impatient demand that they use the stairs instead of waiting for the lift, and Paul's terse reply that they'd only take longer that way. It was still shut when the lift arrived, and Paul bundled her into it.

Then came another jumble of impressions. The flowery streets, lit by white moon and yellow lamps and giving back the ghost of the day's heat. A dark, glossy car which received her with deep-cushioned ease into the rich scent of good leather. A heart-stopping moment when Paul flicked at her skirts, but he was only making sure he didn't close the door on them. Another when he took the driver's seat and leant over her, touching her shoulder and then her thigh through the double-layered skirts, but he was only satisfying himself that her safety-belt wasn't twisted, and was properly closed.

There was absolutely no need for this languor. She mustn't allow these hot little pulses of her blood, which made her feel so exposed and vulnerable even in her most covered, most secret places. It was positively wicked to feel this way, with poor Claudia so ill.

She must try and think about nothing. Just watch the city lights sliding by. Just breathe in this scent of good leather, which had now somehow mixed itself with the scent of wild thyme. Just rub her cheek against this strangely angled pillow, whose cover was for all the world like wool suiting...

'What?' She jerked awake in a new, steady brightness.

'I said we're there.'

'Wh-where? What...? Who...? Oh.' It all came rushing back, and she put a hand to her cheek, still hot from its contact with his shoulder. 'You shouldn't have let me do that.'

But he only got out, and came round to open her door.

After that, it was more jumble. Dazzled in the brightness of the reception area, she waited for Paul to make his rapid enquiries, then let him lead her along polished corridors, past rows of doors, round corners, and through another door.

'Sit.' He was standing before her with hands either side of her waist, pushing her gently downwards.

She sank obediently, and found herself on a wide, padded bench, not the height of comfort but not bad. She settled against its padded back, and opened her eyes. To her dismay Paul was on another, facing her.

'Take off your shoes and put your feet up,' he ordered. 'They say we can have this room to ourselves until morning.'

'But I don't want...not the whole bench...' She stopped and tried again, muzzily determined to explain. 'It's lonely.' She surveyed him in foggy apology. 'There's been such a lot happening...and all so different from home...'

Then somehow he was at her side. His arm held her warm and safe and his fingers pressed lightly on her temple, tipping her head to his shoulder.

'Sleep, then, little green heart. I'll wake you when we're told anything.'

And this was all right, wasn't it? This was fine. You could relax here, warm in the circle of his arms, your head on his shoulder, your nostrils snuffing up the scent of wild thyme and honey, rose-water, marigold-water, flowers gathered towards the east where the bees tended the fragrant pink blossom and filled their own little paniers with honey...

'Hnh?'

She'd meant it to be a noise of enquiry, but it came out a thin little squeak. She sat up, stretched, and consulted her watch. Could that be the hour-hand, pushing towards four? She rubbed her eyes, and it still was.

'Is it really that late?'

'Let's call it early.' His voice was different, lighter, almost smiling. 'Did you hear anything the doctor told us?'

'What doctor?' She blinked round the empty room.

The smile reached his mouth. 'It's going to be all right.'

'Oh, Paul, I'm so glad!' Taffy sprang to her feet in a great rush of pleasure. 'Can we go and see her?'

He shook his head. 'Come back tomorrow, the doctor says. For now...'

He stood up to join her, a sudden blaze of vitality in the white, bare room. Before she knew what was happening, he had seized her waist and whirled her in a dizzy half-circle.

'For now, I want to go out and celebrate.'

'So do I, Paul.' She let him hold her, let the bright world turn and settle while she hung content in his grip. 'So do I.'

She had instinctively grabbed his shoulders for balance. Now her hands knew them, their breadth and hardness, the play of muscles under suit and shirt. She could feel them changing and flexing, yet their message was one of firmness, of steadiness, of a strong centre which would be there when the rest of creation had all whirled to dust.

No, not dust, she couldn't think of dust at this time of delight. Let it be blossom. Let it be a million, billion, trillion fragments of wild thyme scattered on the wind, falling and falling about her...

Or was it she who was falling? Anybody would, with this hard mouth claiming hers. It had stopped being blossom now and become just what it was, a man making love to a woman. Not only his mouth wanted her, but his hands. One lingered at her waist, the other drew sweetness from her bare shoulders with dancing, feathery caresses which brought it, in the most natural, gradual progress in the world, beneath the cotton of her dress and the lace of her bra to the hidden slopes of her breasts.

She gasped, half in longing, half in fright. No man had been here before, she wouldn't allow it, so why was she helpless before this mastering hand? His fingertips settled in a light, tantalising circle, heedless of her pleading.

'Not there, Paul! Not there!'

She didn't even know what she meant by it, but surely not this? Surely not that he should draw away and leave her so untended, so urgent with a longing she barely understood?

But he couldn't leave her, any more than she could let him. His hand rested a moment on her shoulder, then with its own sudden decision pushed down the concealing dress, the supporting strap, and swooped again to its quarry.

And here was her captive breast with its secret clear to his gaze, its untouched bud pink and shameless. His thumb nudged it, challenged it, subdued and released it, and new demand boiled within her until she didn't know how to contain it. She turned her head aside and shut her eyes tight, but it was no use, she couldn't shut it out. When his lips took her breast, her body clenched and unclenched of its own accord, then yielded with a sigh to the engulfing pleasure of his stroking, circling tongue.

She could hardly bear it when he stopped. But this time he didn't mean to go away; his mouth wanted hers, and he had found her other breast to kindle to new peaks of ecstasy so that she had to cling to him. Close, close she pressed to his strength, his hidden fullness which, aeons ago, had so frightened her.

Had she really been frightened of this, and the joyful union it promised? She wasn't now. Her whole body surged towards it like a green thing blindly seeking the sun.

'I...' She took her lips from his, fighting for breath. 'I—never—ever—made love properly—before.'

'Green heart.' His lips moved on her cheek. 'You still haven't.'

'But I didn't... I never...' She shook her head, trying to clear her thoughts. 'Nobody ever made me want to, before.'

'I'm honoured.'

But he didn't act honoured. Instead he put her away from him, and took his hands from her as if he, too, were just waking. Then with a muffled exclamation he pulled her dress roughly to her shoulders, thrust his hands in his pockets, and turned away.

'I'd better get you home.'

'No!' She stared at him, aware of her curls wild about her face, her lips moist with desire. 'I...I could never...it'd be no use me going to bed now...not alone...'

She broke off, realising that she had, after all, said what she wanted to. For a long moment he stared at her, his breathing quickened anew, longing and disbelief warring in the dark eyes.

'My heedless Taffy, you realise what you're saying?'

'I...I know——' she forced herself to face it '—that not every man wants to be the first.'

'I'd be honoured.' That word again, and used so simply. 'But my darling, we only met——' a glance at his own watch, a lightning calculation '—six hours ago.'

'Six very crowded hours.'

'You've slept for most of them.'

'That's part of it.' She broke off, wondering why it should be. 'Ever since we met, I've...liked you——' she lowered her heavy lids, not needing to explain '—but that wouldn't have been enough. It's...it's the way you *care*...that's it! You care.' She stared up at him, triumphant to have cleared her meaning from the tangle within her. 'And because you're a man who counts, your caring counts too.'

'I am what I am.' The dark eyes closed, and opened with a new resolution which tightened the high cheekbones and folded the long mouth to a tight, straight line. 'And I want you very much, Taffy Griffin. But...you mustn't rush into something you might be sorry for.'

'I'll never be sorry,' she declared, convinced of it. 'Not when it's you, Paul.'

He reached out, and softly tucked her disordered hair behind her ears. 'I wish I could be so sure.'

'You can be,' she told him, as positive as she knew how to be. 'Absolutely sure.'

'We'll see.' With sudden resolution, he turned from her and opened the door. 'Listen, Taffy.' He gestured her through it. 'I'm walking you home.'

'You're what?' She didn't move, couldn't believe her ears.

'I'm taking your green English heart for a walk through the green heart of Europe.'

'At four in the morning?'

'It'll be daylight by the time we reach your flat.' He seized her hand and urged her along with him. 'We'll walk through the dawn. After that, if you still want...' He lifted a strand of her hair, and kissed it. 'If you still offer what I so much want, I'll take it.'

Then came another dreamy interlude. Though wide awake this time, she still couldn't have told their route.

She recognised the Avenue de la Liberté, busy even now
with traffic, and the single-span Pont Adolphe above an
airy darkness which in daytime she knew to be the trees
and turf of the steep Pétrusse valley. But how did they
get from the bridge to the rearing fortress of the Bock?
And later, to the pavement outside the Grand Ducal
Palace? And after that, to the bright shops of traffic-
free Grand-Rue? She couldn't have said where they
climbed, where descended, which corners they turned,
which they walked on by.

She did notice when the sky first lightened, above
another green darkness whispering with night sounds.
This turned out to be the Parc de la Ville; she knew it
when they reached the statue of Jean L'Aveugle and the
silent brilliance of roundabouts and sideshows which
filled Glacis Square. By the time they had crossed Glacis
to the darker streets of her own neighbourhood, the sky
had paled through mist-grey to primrose to luminous
blue.

'See those little clouds?' He showed her where they
floated above the roof-tops, mere feathers of light-pink
vapour. 'When you blush, you're exactly that colour.'
He stared at her more closely. 'Are you blushing now,
or is it only the light?'

'I don't know.' She glanced down at the pavement,
up at the sky, across to the man who stood between her
and the world. 'I don't know anything any more, not
where I am, nor who I am...'

'Nor what you're doing?'

'I do know that.'

Did she speak too hastily, too determined to convince
herself? It didn't matter. She knew the one important
thing: that she hadn't changed her mind. She had chosen
to explore the first pleasures of love, and she had chosen

this man to partner her in them. Let the rest take care of itself.

'I know it for sure, now.' She tilted her head back to stare up at him in the blurred softness of the dawn. 'Do you?'

'I always did.' He took out his own keys, and opened the apartment block they had left such a momentous time ago. 'Stairs or lift?'

'I get the choice this time?'

'This time, you get every choice there is.'

'Not quite every...' She swallowed it back. 'Lift, then.'

She hadn't asked for promises, and she didn't need them. She didn't need anything but the here and now, the closed-in brightness of the lift, his arms about her and his lips on hers.

Slowly, they rose to the place where only she could invite him. The place which, once he had entered it, could never be the same again.

As if to acknowledge that, he let her lead him out of the lift, and along to her own door. 'From now on, you're in charge.'

'Am I, Paul?' She stood, uncertain.

'You don't want to be?' His fingers found their way through her hair to dance on the nape of her neck. 'I have to tell you what to do?'

'Tell, and...' She looked away, suddenly shy. 'And show.'

'It will be a pleasure, my darling. A rare pleasure.'

He took her key from her, opened the door, snapped on the hall light, and gestured her in ahead of him. Her little flat greeted her with its not yet familiar scents, held in while she had been away, of another cook's spices, another woman's perfume. While she hesitated in the hall he closed the door, scooped her into his arms, and carried her in exactly the right direction.

'I didn't make my bed.' She stiffened away from him. 'Annette's bed.'

'That, my darling——' he set her on it and drew her close, his breath warm on her cheek '—was never like this.'

She met his eyes, wanting to believe him. 'Wasn't it, Paul? Really never?'

'Really never.' His deep voice made her realise how childish the phrase was, but he didn't seem to mind. 'Did you know your eyes are the exact colour of beech leaves when the sun shines through them?' His hands caressed her back. 'Not now, though. Just now they're huge and dark as the ocean... Let's get rid of this.'

He rose, and dumped the duvet over the foot of the bed. A flick, a shrug, and his jacket had dropped there, too. She revelled in his superb movements against the gold rectangle of the doorway, his tie pulled away from his smooth throat and discarded in its turn, his rangy shoulders clearly outlined in the white, light-gilded shirt.

'No.' He was with her again, pushing the bedside light away before she could switch it on. 'Later, maybe.' In the yellow-striped dimness, he cradled her waist in his two big hands. 'Lean towards me.'

'What?' But she obeyed even as she questioned, and found her dress and bra dropping away. 'How did you do that?'

'I just did.' He stared down, hypnotised, and lifted the weight of her breasts in both hands. 'What treasure.'

And he buried his face in them. She felt the strands of his hair, the little spikes of his lashes, the rasp of his early morning stubble, and then clung to him in ecstasy as he tasted each crest in turn, and again, and again...

'I didn't mean to do that.' He left them at last, ignoring their helpless, flaring signals. 'Not till we're ready.'

'We're . . .' She could hardly breathe, but need drove her. 'We're not ready? What are you doing . . .?'

He had risen, lifting her with him to set her upright before him. While she stammered her bewilderment, he pushed down the dress and bra so mysteriously loosened, the unresisting petticoat and briefs, until they foamed round her naked feet.

'Don't hide.' He captured her instinctively spread hands. 'You're beautiful.' And he kissed her shoulder, the inward curve of her waist, the tops of her impatient breasts, until she struggled to free her hands.

'Let me, Paul. It's not fair . . .'

And then she found her own fingers rejoicing in the edged pearl buttons of his shirt. Flick—flick—flick, the crisp fabric parted, and here were the long hollows and ridges of his shoulders, the dusting of dark hair on the wide chest, and here more hair, down where this belt needed opening . . .

'No.' He put her away from him. 'This part's for me to take care of.'

'Don't!' she cried, bereft as he moved away with his back to her. 'I want . . . I have to . . .'

'No, *I'm* the one who has to.' His other clothes joined the tangled pile at the foot of the bed, but he still kept his back to her, dark head bowed in the muted glow of the distant light.

'What are you *doing*?'

She sank forlorn to the bed, hungry for his closeness. She could feast her eyes from here, revel in the smooth back barred with yellow light, the tanned skin glossy with health, the narrow hips and muscular buttocks and long, supple legs, but it wasn't enough. Only *he* would be enough, now.

Now and forever. The words floated into her mind, and she almost managed to thrust them aside, but not quite. They wouldn't quite go. They meant a lot, those words, and not only to herself. They had to be dealt with, and perhaps now, while his back was turned, was the best time.

'Paul.' She saw his head slant to a listening angle, and pushed the words out fast, before she could lose her courage. 'I know it's over with Annette, and I know it's...' She faced him, and pushed on. 'That it's all right about Claudia. But what about...?'

She had to stop here. He was with her at last, a warmth and a closeness sweeping her down into the half-dark. She struggled away from him, bracing her arms to hold him off.

'You're not... being unfaithful to anyone?'

'Of course not!' He stilled in astonishment. 'Do you think I'd be here if I were?'

'I know you're not married, or even engaged...'

'I most certainly am not!'

'But there's no other woman you've been seeing? No woman who's hoping——?'

'None.' He pushed aside her guarding arms, and tumbled her with him to the mattress. 'Haven't you left it a bit late to ask that?'

'Better late than never... What are you doing?' She threw her head back with a shudder of pleasure. 'Don't stop...'

But he went his own way, at his own speed. He spun her on uprushes of longing, engulfed her in tides of desire that lapped now one part of her, now another. She felt them wash ever higher, ever hotter, until her drowning senses begged for she knew not what.

'Now, Paul, please, please...'

His lips came down on hers, silencing her. But her inner clamour wouldn't be silenced; it sent her arching and straining towards him, demanding that flowering which only his sunlight could achieve in her, the wholeness only he could complete.

And so his fullness sought hers, and found it.

CHAPTER FOUR

'TAFFY!' Paul knocked on the bathroom door. 'Are you all right in there?'

'I'm fine.'

Taffy crouched lower to avoid the daisy-patterned curtains, then sprang up and whipped them wide apart. The red morning sunlight dazzled in, as bright as if this were the best day of her life instead of the worst. She belted tighter the robe she had snatched from its hook when she first came in here, and slid once more to the bath-mat.

'Then come on out.' The deep voice on the other side of the door sounded both impatient and concerned. 'I promise you, it won't always be like that.'

Wedged between hard floor, hard wall, and hard bath, she blinked a tear off the end of her lashes. 'Go away.'

'What?' A silence while he took it in. 'Have you gone mad?'

The tear had dropped on her aquamarine towelling sleeve. For a brief moment it sparkled there, orange-gold in the new-risen sun, then sank away to a tiny, round damp patch. How like life, Taffy decided with distant, dismal satisfaction.

'Come out of there and talk.' He rattled the door-handle.

'What's the good of that?' she demanded furiously.

'You sound as though you think I've done something dreadful,' Paul said, exasperation in every vibrant, muffled note.

'You have!'

66

'If you think that...' He broke off with a small explosion of irritation. 'This is silly. Come out of there at once!'

'No.'

But she found she was sitting straighter, feeling better. No thanks to him, though, she told herself fiercely. She would never, ever forgive him for the way he had chosen to keep his distance from her.

'Just go.' Her words echoed from the tiled walls with far more vigour than she intended, and she hastily toned down the volume. 'And don't come back.'

'Of all the half-baked, senseless... Listen to me.' His voice suddenly took on that familiar, steely authority. 'If you don't open this door, I'll break it in.'

'You couldn't. People don't do that in real life.' She felt better than ever at being able to show her superior wisdom. 'All it breaks is your shoulder. Even yours,' she added, a picture flashing into her mind of those wide, naked shoulders.

'I wouldn't shoulder-charge it, idiot. I'd smash this——' his fist thumped the door's light upper panel '—then reach in and unbolt it.'

'You'd mess your hand up worse than your shoulder.'

'So I would,' he responded, light and drawling.

'Still, it's your hand,' she added. 'Feel free.'

No answer.

'It's your property, too,' she added on a new wave of wretchedness. 'Even if I'm not.'

And he didn't want her to be—he'd proved that effectively. She huddled lower, remembering what should have been the supreme moment of union, and how it had turned into nothing but disappointment. That *was* all his fault! Well, he could just go away, out of her life and never come back.

Why wasn't he answering—and what was that?

She strained forward, listening. Yes, her ears weren't playing tricks, those really were his footsteps padding away down the hall. There went the bedroom door; she recognised the soft grating sound where it fitted too close to the carpet. He must have gone to put his clothes on.

So he was leaving, just because she'd told him to. The lousy quitter! Why, he'd hardly even begun to *try* arguing her out of here. All he'd done was threaten a little, and he'd thought better of that the minute she reminded him he'd be damaging his own property. What a materialist!

'I might have known,' she shouted as loud as she could. 'You're as careful about goods as you are about love.'

No answer. Probably he couldn't even hear, but, if he could, he still wouldn't bother. Why should he? He'd taken his safe pleasure, and was now proving, if proof were needed, how little she meant to him.

'At least I found you out in time,' Taffy shouted, and curled tight into herself with her arms round her knees.

If only it were true! If only she had found out really in time, before she rushed into this experience that had changed her forever, this love-*game* which had just finished so painfully. If only she hadn't been so impulsive, so carried away with the crowded events of the past few hours, so thrilled with that early morning walk in the city.

He'd said it was to give her time to think, that walk. But all it had done was draw her ever deeper into the illusion that he was the man for her. And all the time he knew quite well that she wasn't the only woman for him. Knew it so well that he...

No, she wouldn't think of it. She would just sit here and think about nothing. There were his steps again, padding out of the bedroom and along the corridor. In a minute he'd be gone, the front door would close, and she could come out and try to start living again in the empty, miserable world.

But he hadn't left—here were his footsteps returning, still muffled but light and purposeful, from wherever they had been. 'Listen to me, Taffy.' His voice was purposeful, too. 'I have here a rather fetching bronze lady——'

'My gym prize!' She shot to her feet, banging her elbow sharply on the towel-rail. 'How dare you?' she fumed, nursing it in her other hand. 'How dare you go into my living-room, and help yourself to——?'

'I dare more than that. Are you coming out?'

'Put my prize back, this minute!'

'You can have it when I've broken in the panel.'

'No!' She had the door unbolted before she realised she'd done it, and flew at him, and snatched the bronze figure close to her aquamarine-towelled bosom. 'I never won any after this, I got to be the wrong shape...' She stopped, as angry now with herself as with him.

And, of course, trust him to make the most of it. 'So how did you manage to be the wrong shape for gym?'

'In the normal way,' she snapped. 'I grew up.'

'You did? I'd never have guessed.'

'That's right, make fun of me now you've——' she sought for a suitable expression '—now you've taken my all...' As soon as the melodramatic phrase was out, she could have kicked herself.

Sure enough, the dark features lit with mockery. 'That was your all? It wasn't much, was it, dormouse?'

She whirled to face him, horrified. 'You mean I'm no good? *You're* disappointed?'

'You're surely not expecting congratulations?'

'How can you be so cruel?' she gulped, new tears threatening. 'As if it wasn't bad enough already...'

'Come on, you're not making sense.' He lifted an outer curl of the tangled mass on her collar, and let it twirl round his finger. 'How could I possibly be happy that you're upset?'

'I don't see why not.' She flounced the curl out of his grasp and turned away from him, digging her bare heel into the carpet. 'You're the one who decided it would be like that.'

'Calm down, dormouse!'

'I'm as calm as anything,' she gulped, defying that response to his near-touch which had spread like inner fire to her scalp. 'I have decided——' she set off for the living-room '—in the calmest possible manner, that I don't want to see you again. Not ever,' she added, as much for herself as for him.

'So I'm to be cast off like a worn-out glove?'

She ignored him, reaching the display shelves and putting her precious bronze carefully back in place. That left her free to pay attention to her aching elbow, which she made a great show of nursing as she turned back to look at him.

This, she realised, was the first time she'd really seen him since she came out of the bathroom. He had indeed dressed, or partly. He hadn't yet bothered with shoes and socks, and his feet showed darkly tanned in the light filtering through the still closed green curtains. He had pulled on his fine-tailored trousers all anyhow, and his crumpled shirt flopped tieless from his strong throat. The hair which had been so perfectly combed now swirled over his forehead and ears, with a tuft at the crown standing determinedly upright.

Taffy gulped. Why was it specially exciting to see this well-groomed man in such casual disarray? She longed to cross to where he lounged so superbly against the doorpost, longed just to reach up in the filtered green light, and press down that obstinate crown-tuft. Her fingers remembered the stiffness of it, the way it had prickled into them such a short time ago...

She thrust her hands in her pockets. 'It was all,' she announced firmly, 'a terrible mistake.'

'Pity.' His insolent glance flicked over her belted-in curves. 'You may be the wrong shape for gym, but for what I have in mind at the moment...' He sauntered over to her.

She kept her hands in her pockets, the nails digging into the palms. 'If...if what you have in mind at the moment,' she echoed, 'is...is what you did before, then you can forget it. I,' she added, contradicting the clamour of her blood, 'have lost all interest.'

'You have?' he drawled, and caught her to him.

The humiliating part was that she didn't even struggle. She got her hands out of her pockets in time, and set them on the crumpled shirt to hold him off, but they wouldn't. The minute her fingers felt that great warm chest, they went their own way, first to the broad, shirt-covered shoulders, then to the strong neck, and at last into the stiff hair where they wanted to be. And she had to let them rejoice in its stiffness, exactly as her lips were rejoicing in the hardness of his.

It was he who ended the kiss, in his own good time. When he put her away from him he was breathing a little fast, but he soon mastered that.

'Naturally the choice is yours,' he murmured almost evenly. 'But I'm pretty sure you haven't quite finished with me yet.'

'Then you're wrong.' She flung away from him, dry-mouthed. 'I'm never going to speak to you again, let alone get back into bed with you.'

He greeted the news with one of his formal bows, brief and full of mockery. 'Just as you like,' he answered equably. 'But before you start never speaking to me again, you'd better tell me what's eating you.'

'You never cared about me one little bit.'

'Interesting.' His hand closed on her elbow, drawing her round to face him.

'Don't!' She exaggerated her yelp of pain. 'You've hurt me there. Look!' She pulled back her wide sleeve, and, since her elbow showed no sign of injury, pointed dramatically. 'I'll have a bruise there tomorrow.'

'Shame.' He inspected the place with teasing concern. 'And when did I do this?'

'Just now. In the bathroom.'

'Naughty me.' With a swift, graceful movement, he dropped to one knee and set his lips to her elbow. 'There,' he murmured, rising to his feet as she snatched it away. 'All better?'

'I am not a child!' she raged. 'And it *was* your fault, so you needn't pretend to be humouring me.'

'It was, it was,' he soothed, stroking her hair.

'Leave me alone!' She turned away to hide the fresh tremors that were running through her, from her elbow, from her hair. 'To think,' she reminded them both, 'how all during that lovely walk, you were planning...'

'I certainly was. And imagining, too.' His hand closed gently on her upper arm, well clear of the sore elbow, and drew her resistingly round to face him. 'And you know what, dormouse?' He had possession of both her arms now. 'You're going to be better than any of it. Better than anything I could have imagined.'

'Let me go!' She struggled uselessly, weakly, almost overwhelmed by those imprisoning hands.

He kept hold of her. 'Not till you tell me what's wrong.'

'You know damn well what's wrong!'

'Cry-baby.' The dark eyes took on a wicked glint. 'Come back to bed, and I'll kiss that better, too.'

She felt the hairs rise on the back of her neck, and realised that her mouth had dropped foolishly open. No, not foolishly, or not only that... She closed it tight, fighting off the languor he could still so easily rouse in her.

'You're hateful,' she whispered fiercely. 'Quite hateful, to talk as if it were nothing.'

'All right, so it was upsetting when it happened. But don't tell me that you're still angry.' He ran that dark, penetrating gaze over her face. 'Because I can see that you're not.'

She was further incensed to realise that he was right. Well, he needn't think it would make any difference.

'So you know how I feel better than I do myself?'

'No, but I do have eyes.' He rode down her attempt to interrupt. 'Your colour's back, pink as a rose.'

She jerked her head to one side, refusing the compliment. The sudden movement bounced her hair over her face and she left it there, instinctively hiding. Thus shut off from him, she was completely taken by surprise when he gently parted the two lapels of her robe.

'Pink as...' Under her outraged gaze he lifted her breasts in both hands, the tip of his tongue stealing out between the white teeth. 'I was going to say strawberries and cream, but these are better.'

'L-leave me alone!'

She snatched the robe together, and hastily retreated to the other side of the coffee-table. He moved after her, and she cast round for a weapon to hold him off. Here it was, the Cinderella-slipper he'd returned to her last night. She grabbed its furry upper, and waved its sharp heel as threateningly as she could.

'If you get any nearer, I'll...' She broke off with a little scream as he wrenched it from her hand and threw it hard across the room. 'What the hell do you think you're doing? You nearly broke my lamp.'

'I did exactly what I meant to do.'

He swooped to the coffee-table and seized the other object lying there, the little torn-off green button. A swift, dextrous twist of the strong wrist, and he had fired it with deadly accuracy at the preening neck of the china-swan lamp. It hit with an echoing tinkle, and dropped harmlessly to the floor.

Taffy rushed over to check her swan for damage. Finding none, she drew the curtains and checked again in the sunlight. Still none, but that surely couldn't have been what he intended.

'First my gym prize, now my swan.' She stayed where she was with her back to the window, drawn up in righteous wrath. 'Are you trying to break up my home the way you've broken my...?'

Heart, she'd meant to say, but stopped herself in time. There was no question, she told herself, of his ever having been that important to her, and he needn't think it.

But he wasn't thinking in that direction at all. She could see it in his eyes, alight once more with wicked humour. He'd expected her to say something quite different, and she wouldn't put it past him to say it for her.

However, he only nodded at the abused slipper. 'Were you, or were you not, threatening me with that thing?' He grinned. 'For someone so upset, you have plenty of fight in you, dormouse!'

'What else can I do, if you won't take no for an answer?'

'Consider it taken.'

But he still crossed to her in one easy stride. She stepped hastily backwards, stumbled over the wretched slipper, and would have fallen against the window if he hadn't caught her.

'Watch it.' He kept his steadying hands either side of her waist. 'We don't want me smashing your window along with my other crimes, do we?'

'It would have been your fault, same as the rest...'

'That's enough.' He manhandled her into a safer part of the room, his hands staying warm and firm on her waist. 'You'd better tell me what's bothering you.'

She hesitated. Somehow it didn't seem nearly so bad, now that the pain had stopped and he was holding her like this.

'You're going to tell me. Or you know what?' His arms stole round her. 'I'll take you back to the bedroom, and make love to you again.'

'With more precautions?' Her rage came back in full force at the memory. 'When we stopped at that all-night shop, I'd no idea what you were buying.'

'So, that's it!' The splendid, tousled head tilted, waiting.

'And when we were undressing, and you wouldn't let me...' She floundered, hating to recreate that moment when he had put her away from him, and turned his back, and not told her what he was doing. 'When you wouldn't...come straight to bed with me,' she struggled on, 'I'd no idea what...what it was all about.' She warmed to her grievance. 'I only found out afterwards.'

'Let me get this straight.' Indulgence slowly fading from the dark eyes, he dropped his arms, and put a tiny, telling fraction of extra distance between her body and his. 'Are you really saying that all this fuss is because I took care of you?'

'No! But because you didn't share it with me...' she stormed, letting it all pour out now she'd started. 'I sud-

denly realised that this was an everyday occurrence for
you!'

'And how do you know that?' He gripped her
shoulders, ready to shake an answer out of her.

She wouldn't meet his eyes. 'Take your hands off me.'

To her surprise, he did. She remembered the last time
he'd let her go so abruptly, on the balcony of his flat
after their first kiss, and felt a tremor of fear. Was he
angry with her now, as he'd been then?

She stole a glance at him, and found the dark eyes
opaque, the rugged features set as carved stone. She felt
her own tension mount, and moved with careful steps
out of his reach.

'There must be some sense in this somewhere,' he
began in a low, controlled growl. 'You must have some
better reason than you've just given, for carrying on like
this.'

'I am not *carrying on*,' she flared. 'I'm just...just
miserable, that's all.'

'Miserable like a sick frog.'

'What?' She felt her eyes widen, her mouth gape with
outrage. 'What a horrible thing to say!'

'It's not a good thing to have about, either.'

'I do not in the least resemble a...' Her tongue almost
refused to shape the insult. 'A frog!'

'No?' The dark eyes swept over her. 'You should see
yourself. Your lower lip's been tripping you up ever since
I got you out of there.' He indicated the bathroom with
a jerk of his head, and went on in that menacing growl.
'Let's try it once more. Exactly why have you been
playing up?'

'I haven't been...' She caught his eye, and hurried
on. 'I told you, I...you...' She sought desperately for
another way of putting it. 'You...you deliberately chose

to keep me in the dark. That told me that I meant nothing special to you.'

He let her stumble to a silence that went on and on. He was staring down at her with a frown like gathering thunder, ever more threatening. When he next spoke, it was out of a stillness heavy with menace.

'You'd rather I'd risked your having a baby?'

'Th-there you go again,' she stammered, doing her best with a voice that wouldn't quite obey her. 'Do you have to be so...so earthy?'

'There's nothing earthier than pregnancy, I'm told. Unless it's——'

'Don't!' She clapped her hands over her ears, so hard that her head rang. 'I don't want to hear any more of this.'

'You'd rather experience it?' The words hissed between his clenched teeth, yet easily penetrated her useless efforts to keep them out. 'Do you think these things go away because you don't care to hear about them?'

'You're not trying to understand how I feel at all.' She dropped her hands from her ears, and clasped them in front of her. 'When you didn't tell me what you were doing, it was as if you didn't trust me...'

'Trust you!'

The words exploded out of him with such force that she took a step backwards, and overbalanced into the big armchair. She sat there petrified, not daring to look up in case she should see him outlined in fiery sparks like Lucifer.

'You damned silly little...' He stopped, dragged in a deep breath, and started again. 'Are you perhaps under the impression that *trust*——' more sparks as he spat out the word '—is a form of birth-control?'

She kept her head down, not venturing a reply.

'No? Then perhaps you fancied starting a baby?'

Her head jerked up at that. 'Of course not!'

'Are you sure? You wouldn't be the first woman to try and land a rich husband that way.'

She was on her feet before he'd finished, fists clenched, hair bouncing on her collar. 'How can you be so vile?'

'I'm not saying you're clever enough to work it out.' The sparks had faded, leaving a tempered-steel calm in their place. 'But it could be there just the same, in that unformed little mind of yours.'

'It wasn't! I swear it wasn't!' She struggled against tears which somehow seemed more real than any that had gone before. 'I'd never even *think* of such a thing!'

She found she couldn't see him properly, and searched her pockets frantically for a handkerchief. He pulled out his own and offered it, snowy white, immaculately folded—and with Annette Warren's gold chain, carelessly shoved away last night, coiled within it like a snake round its poison-bright coral heart.

So that was why he was willing to suspect her of something so awful. White and coral and gold all blurred together in Taffy's vision, then separated as he let the bauble fall, shook out the handkerchief with a snap, and all but threw it at her.

'Th-thanks.' She buried her face in it, glad to hide in its wild-thyme fragrance. 'W-would *she*——' Taffy stirred with her toe the cold coral and gold on the carpet '—have done something like that?'

'Leave Annette out of this.'

'I c-can't. She's m-made you all s-suspicious and horrible, and now you won't believe me...'

'What does it matter?' And he really sounded as if it didn't. 'You're either playing up, or playing for high stakes—what's the difference?'

'All the difference in the world!'

She lowered the handkerchief from her face and almost held it out to him, a pleading white flag. One glance at the stony, unmoving figure, the carved, rock-hard features, showed how useless that would be.

She suddenly longed for the sexual appetite which a minute ago had shown her the inner fullness of that unyielding mouth. Even the teasing kindness which had so irritated her, even the mockery would have been welcome now, she realised with a pang.

'How could you believe I'd do such a thing?' She looked down at the green water patterns of the carpet, across the sunlit street, anywhere but at him. 'We...I thought we were in...' She trailed off, not able to speak the word.

'In love?' he finished, careless of her feelings. 'You really think you're ready for that?'

'P-please, Paul!' She crushed the handkerchief between her two hands. 'Please don't s-spoil it all...'

'You're asking *me* not to spoil it?' He stared down at her in contemptuous disbelief. 'You don't think *your* little tantrum might have spoilt anything?'

'I only——'

'You only ran off without a word, at the very time when we should have been most together...' But now it was his turn to break off, his mouth hardening as if against a weakness.

She stared at him in bewilderment. 'It was no good our being together. It hurt me to realise that our being together was nothing special for you.'

'What a fool you are!' He turned abruptly away from her, and padded across to the door.

'I don't understand.' She followed him down the corridor. 'How would it have helped if I'd stayed with you?'

He strode before her into the bedroom. There, in the underwater light of the closed curtains, he went to the tumbled clothes and bed-linen on the carpet. A pull, a twist, and his tie landed on the bed, quickly followed by socks and jacket. He threw his shoes one by one to the floor by the bed and straightened, still with that frightening, impassive mask.

'Out of my way.' He brushed past her, sat on the bed, and quickly pulled on his socks.

Taffy felt her lips quiver. 'You're g-going? Like th-this?'

'Like you told me to, yes.'

'But I d-didn't mean——'

'Didn't mean me to, no,' he cut in with brutal candour. 'I was supposed to stay and pet you out of your mood, like you're used to.'

'How the hell do you know what I'm used to?' she demanded, goaded to retaliate.

He gave her a brief, dismissive glance, and went back to fastening his shoelaces. 'It's in everything you say and do. It's even in the way you look.' He took up the silvery tie, its network of fine green overchecks invisible now in the filtered light, and sauntered to her dressing-table. 'You're spoilt rotten.' He stooped to the mirror, and put on the tie with quick, decisive movements. 'By your parents, I expect.'

'That's not true.' But she had to speak extra loud, to cover her misery at the too-familiar words. 'My parents had a pub to run, and three other children.'

'They still managed to give you far too much of your own way.' His reflection threw her another of those chill, withering glances. 'Being the only girl, I suppose.'

Other men had told her similar things, and it hadn't mattered. This time, she was glad she hadn't managed to return his handkerchief, needing it to scrub away fresh tears.

'You s-said we w-were going to b-b-be better than anything you c-could ever have imagined...'

'So we were, dormouse, so we were.' But he spoke briskly, brushing by her once more to shrug into his jacket. 'Until you decided I was a criminal.'

'I n-never s-said you were a c-criminal.' She blinked, and sniffed hard, forcing herself to try and explain one more time. 'Only that...what you did...doesn't seem to go with being in...' It was no use, she still couldn't say it.

'In love?' he finished for her, ruthless as before, and shrugged. 'I was certainly attracted. I always did have a weakness for curvy, creamy...'

He broke off. She had looked up, hope renewed by the words and by the warmth that had crept into his voice, but he only turned abruptly away from her.

'To think I was even enjoying petting you!'

He took a comb from an inner pocket, and reduced his wiry hair to order. Though he wasn't using the mirror now, his hair obeyed him at once, and Taffy, watching, knew how it felt. In this mood, he got his own way, or else.

'Ah, well.' Almost as impeccable as when she'd first seen him, he put away the comb with an air of finality. 'At least I found you out in time.'

She recognised with dismay the very words she herself had shouted, unheard, through the bathroom door. The difference was, she hadn't meant them, and he did. She gathered her strength for one final, desperate plea.

'You can't believe I wanted to...' Her voice almost failed on the ugly word, but she managed to bring it out. 'To trap you into marriage?'

'Forget it, dormouse. As I shall.'

He'd found some small object in the pocket where he returned the comb. He brought it out, a thing so tiny she couldn't see it properly before his fingers covered it. He weighed it in his closed hand, and then, for the first time since they'd come into this room, really looked at her.

She wanted to shrink away from the shrewd, deep-set eyes, but she withstood them. 'I can't forget it. It's important.'

Another brief, unendurably long survey. She felt as if he were seeing right through her, right into the workings of her mind, but so much the better. She met his eyes unflinchingly, willing him to see the truth.

'All right.' Still he kept up that penetrating stare. 'You're a royal pain in the neck, but you're not a schemer.'

'Oh, thank you, Paul!' she breathed as though he'd paid her the highest compliment, and in the rush of relief and gratitude, threw her arms round his neck.

She never knew quite what she had in mind. To rest her wet, hot cheek against him, perhaps, and be near one last time to that great, alien strength. But when his lips sought hers she gave them freely, and, when he pulled her to that hidden, springing fullness she was only now beginning to understand, she welcomed it, and matched it, and felt her body preparing to receive it.

But he didn't want her, not really. Already he had taken his lips from hers, and dropped his arms from around her, and put her away from him. And when he took her hand, it wasn't in love or even in friendship, but only to turn it palm upward so he could drop something in it.

'Here.' Hoarse but controlled, he stepped back from her. 'You'd better have that.'

She stared down, and found it was the missing green button from her négligé. 'You said you didn't collect trophies.'

He turned to leave, not letting her see his face. 'I just couldn't help...' He cleared his throat and started anew, iron-cold, already on his way to the front door. 'I don't. That's why I gave it back.'

She followed him. 'You didn't give Annette her heart back.'

'To hell with Annette's heart.'

He moved to the door, and opened it. In a strengthening wave of fury she raised her arm and threw the button at him with all her force. She didn't know whether to be glad or sorry when it missed, and bounced off the wall. He didn't even look to see where it had fallen, only turned back to her with a grim smile.

'There, there. Better now?'

'I wonder what you'll get from the next girl who moves in here?'

'You're leaving?'

'I'm certainly not staying on here.'

'Good.' He put his hand to the outer catch of the door. 'I swear I'll personally vet the next tenant.'

'You fancy a brunette, perhaps?'

'I fancy some peace. No women under fifty.'

He closed the door, but he needn't think he was going to get away with the last word like that. She rushed to it, tore it open, and shouted after him down the stairs.

'That's exactly what you need, someone the same mental age as you are.'

'Whereas you——' he paused on the half-landing '—need somebody aged sixteen. No, that's too mature, better make it——'

She banged the door before he'd finished, and retreated as far as she could get from him, which meant into the living-room. And there it still lay scattered about, the wreckage of her night, the wreckage of her heart. A

green slipper, a green button, a gold chain with a coral
heart...

To leave this, of all things! She picked it up, its hateful
shiny coldness draping itself about her fingers, and
dropped it in the waste-paper basket. But no, that
wouldn't do, she must put it where she wouldn't see it...

Her doorbell! All over again, her blood leapt. He'd
come back for it. Or—the idea brought her head up,
tense with longing—maybe he'd come back for *her*.
Maybe he meant to say he was sorry, and to let her say
she was sorry too. Then maybe they could start again...

But when she rushed to the open door, it was Nick
who stood there, lanky and untidy and hopeful in the
grey, diffused light of the landing which never saw the
sun.

CHAPTER FIVE

'YOU'RE sure you can get it right this time?' Taffy shouted.

You had to shout, to be heard in this part of the fair. What with excited children of every age and nationality, and hurdy-gurdy music, and sideshow barkers, and the whistles and bumps and trundles of the various hair-raising rides, it was hard to think, let alone talk.

'Just do what I tell you,' Nick bellowed, 'and leave the rest to me.'

Which was much what he'd said the first three times, but she was too weary to argue. She heaved herself once more to the white roundabout horse, and arranged herself as gracefully as possible on its gilded, jewel-painted saddle. Scents of hot food wafted up to her, of spicy sausages, and fresh bread, and—would that sharpness be mustard, or was it pickle? And why was she so interested, when she was too miserable ever to want food again?

The morning had passed in a daze. She'd showered, and changed into this cool, simple cotton shift, and tidied her flat, and hated the telephone for not ringing, and written to all her friends at home about the exciting time she was having, and hated the telephone, and eaten a tiny wedge of Camembert, and hated the telephone. At last she'd found herself counting the minutes to the fair's opening-time, when she would at least have the distraction of helping with Nick's video.

Not that it was distracting her much after all. How dared Paul Seyler call her a royal pain in the neck? She

hated him. No, it was herself she hated, for her un-
thinking haste, her greed for pleasure, her impulsive sur-
render to temptation. No wonder it had all ended so
badly. She'd made herself cheap, cheap, cheap, and she
ought at least to have been grateful to him for his good
sense in protecting them both.

'*Je m'excuse, mademoiselle.*'

A polite schoolgirl scrambled past Taffy to the next
horse. A pair of younger children tried to board the white
and gilt carriage where Nick was kneeling with his
camera, and were gently repelled by his taciturn hired
sound-technician. The roundabout was filling for the
next ride.

'Cheer up!' Nick called. 'At least try and look as if
you're having fun.'

Heaven forbid that they should have to do this a fourth
time. Taffy flung her head back, and bared her teeth in
what she hoped was a smile at the white and gilt carved
cherub balanced on the carriage. It had its back to her,
but then so had the whole world except for wretched
Nick and his over-complicated camera.

Even when he got the footage he wanted, he seemed
to have only the vaguest idea of what he would do with
it. He could show it at his college video club, but his
babble of selling it, Taffy had slowly realised, was just
silly.

He simply didn't know enough about what he was
doing. He should have used his own camcorder, instead
of hiring all this expensive equipment plus skilled help
at Sunday rates. She didn't know what had gone wrong
with the three earlier shots, but she could guess by the
sound-technician's pointing gestures and businesslike
Luxembourgish explanations before the start of this
fourth attempt.

Nick shrugged them off. 'Claudia was going to wear white, to match the horses,' he lamented. 'And she bought that wig because it's the exact colour of the gilding...'

The music began, cutting him mercifully short. Taffy couldn't have answered except, as she already had several times, that she wasn't Claudia.

She doubted if Claudia would have worn the wig either, in this heat. As for this going round and round and up and down yet again, the only thing to do was to keep your back straight and your teeth bared, and let the brilliance of Glacis Square blur yet again into a spin of colour before your dried-out, burning eyes, and tell your stomach to behave itself.

'Is that it, then?' she asked when at last she could clamber thankfully down.

'It'll have to be,' Nick announced with an air of great efficiency. 'We've got to get on to the big wheel.'

'Nick, I can't.' She allowed herself one glance towards the great wheel with its swinging gondolas. 'I... I don't feel too good.'

'Not you as well!' He flung back his too long hair. 'For heaven's sake, what's the matter with all you women?'

'Maybe if I could rest somewhere...'

'We haven't time, I want to have finished with the wheel before the shepherds come by... Are you all right?' Nick's bossy trumpeting changed to alarm. 'Oh, lord...'

Taffy was aware of his dismayed blue eyes, and of the technician's grimness softening to kindly concern. Then she had to turn away in case her churning, rebellious stomach carried out the showdown it threatened. Did all these whizzes and whirrs and whoops and howls come from the fairground, or were some of them now happening inside her?

She still hadn't worked it out when a blessedly strong arm caught her waist, and drew her to a blessedly strong frame.

'Right, dormouse, I've got you.'

She wondered if she was imagining the blessedly deep notes. They certainly seemed to vibrate right through her, like music in a dream. What were these dreamy words they were shaping now, somewhere in the air over her head?

'Can't you tell she's going to be sick?'

Taffy struggled to free herself. 'I am not!'

It didn't come out quite as definite as she meant it to. In fact to her own ears it sounded more like the high-pitched cheeping of a distressed bird, but at least it caught Paul Seyler's attention. He held her a little away from him.

'You're sure of that?'

'How could I be sick?' she reasoned, forcing her voice down to a breathy groan. 'I haven't eaten anything.'

He held her with humiliating ease, even sparing a hand to cup her chin so that he could examine her face. 'Since when?'

'That's got nothing to do with anything.' Seeing she couldn't shake him off, she let her heavy lids fall to shut him out. 'The point is, my stomach is quite empty, so it couldn't possibly...'

He'd stopped listening, she realised indignantly. Instead, he'd started shouting to Nick over her head. She thought they must be talking English, but in the shrieking pinkness behind her eyelids it was hard to be sure.

Nick was arguing, you could tell from his tone. Maybe he lost the argument. At any rate, when she opened her eyes he wasn't there any more.

'Now, dormouse.' Still Paul Seyler held her, walking her through the crowd with him. 'I'd like to take you to my favourite restaurant, and feed you *Judd matt Gaardebounen*——'

'It would stick in my throat,' she muttered, stiff-legged with the effort of keeping her knees from buckling.

'—but this is an emergency.' Presumably he hadn't even heard her. 'So you're going to have a *Thüringer*, right here.'

'I don't want...' She broke off as she found herself under a red and white striped awning, and snuffed up one of the scents which had so tantalised her on the roundabout. 'What's a *Thüringer*?'

'You'll see.'

And she did. The sausages arrived smoking hot in split crusty rolls, and somehow hers disappeared while he was still only halfway through his. She stared down at her empty paper serviette, wondering what she had meant to say a minute ago.

Ah, yes. That a single bite would choke her.

Here came her second chance—he'd ordered her another. She opened her mouth to refuse, but there the food was under her eager nose, and here she was biting into it before she could stop herself. This time she could really taste it, and never had spices been so subtly blended, nor meat so perfectly browned, nor bread crackled so meltingly on the tongue.

'Feeling better?' He crushed his own paper wrapper, and dropped it in the bin.

She nodded, busy with the last mouthful. Only after she had swallowed it did the fairground come back into focus, and then she was astonished at how much it had changed. Its colours no longer hurt her eyes, nor its separate noises her ears. Instead they wove together into a giant, blissful pattern, a comfortable background to talk against, or anyway, to shout against.

'Much better, thank you.' She could shout quite easily now, which was just as well seeing how much she had to say. 'Er...'

'Yes?' He was waiting for her to go on, her deliverer, the man who had transformed her world.

'Just—er—thanks,' she shouted. 'I didn't know food could make such a difference.'

'I bet you never had to think about it before.'

'Not...not very much...'

But it was no good, she couldn't think about it now either. Not now she was back with Paul Seyler. Not for him the open-necked shirts of the tourists, the efficient blouson of the sound-technician, or Nick's arty tunic. On this hot Sunday afternoon he stayed formal and supernaturally cool in his dark suit, white shirt and quiet tie. Taffy drank in the arrogant movements of the smooth-brushed head and thought of Lucifer, a Prince of Darkness among the summer-holiday crowds...

Fearing to lose her new-found strength, she dropped her second paper serviette into the bin after his, and wondered where to begin. How to choose, from all the questions she wanted to ask, which to express of all the ideas crowding her mind? Perhaps she'd better start with the most important.

'I'm sorry, Paul.'

The arched eyebrows rose. 'Sorry for what, exactly?'

In this brilliant light she could see the complex colours of his eyes, warm brown raying out from the pupil into darkest grey. A brown like amber, a grey like iron, the bright and the dark, the gentle and the hard—which was she to believe?

She looked away, tracing a pattern on the asphalt with the point of her open-toed sandal. 'For playing up, I suppose.'

'Playing up about what?' he persisted, his voice bright-edged, dark-hearted.

She sighed, realising he wasn't going to let her off a thing. 'About...you know...' She dared his eyes, and found them still iron-dark. 'About you being sensible,' she finished in a rush. 'Other things too, but that was the worst.'

'It's the only one I want you to be sorry for.'

She glanced up with the confused feeling of an amber warmth which had somehow got into his voice, too. Sure enough his eyes, still strikingly dark in the lean face, had a new vividness which made it easy for her to go on.

'There's more, though, isn't there?' she began in a careful shout. 'The fuss I made...'

'You haven't taken vows of silence, dormouse. If you're upset, why not fuss?'

'Because it's babyish,' she admitted for the first time in her life. 'Specially carrying on as if it was all your fault.'

'I did have a little something to do with it.'

'Not really. And this——' she held up her bruised elbow '—was all my own doing.'

'Poor dormouse.'

He was laughing at her again, she realised with delight. Why hadn't she understood earlier that when you laughed at people it was because you liked them? He liked her enough to laugh at, and she asked for nothing better. Except perhaps this, being caught to his side in the circle of one strong arm, and sauntering with him through crowds grown infinitely quieter and more manageable.

'That reminds me,' she began as they passed the white and gold roundabout, 'where on earth did you spring from just now?'

He shrugged. 'Everybody comes to Glacis for the Sunday of the *Scheuberfouer*.'

'Even people without children?'

'Some have children, others have Nick.'

'So that's why you're here?' She craned sideways to look up at the etched profile. 'To see how Nick's getting on?'

'You could say that.' He urged her forward. 'His mother expects me to keep an eye on him.'

'So why did you send him away, and take me to eat sausages?'

'Your need was greater.' His guiding hand pressed hard into her waist, but presently relaxed. 'Starving yourself!'

'I wasn't hungry,' she protested. 'Or at least,' she added, shamefaced, 'I didn't think I was.'

His eyes stayed ahead, choosing their route through the shifting crowds. 'I didn't eat much lunch myself today, but at least I tried.'

'So did I try...' She broke off, doing her best to work out the meaning of what he had just said and still keep pace with his long stride. 'Weren't you hungry either?'

'Careful!' He steered her round a small girl with a huge ice-cream. 'Do you want to go on the big wheel?'

'No, thank you.' She planted her feet apart, refusing to go further and forcing an oncoming pushchair to swerve round them. 'Why weren't you hungry?'

He turned reluctantly to face her, a rearing darkness against the bright lights, the bright sky, the bright holiday crowds. For a moment she didn't know which aspect of him she was going to see, the iron or the amber.

Then he smiled. 'So I'm to talk about it here? An extra sideshow, free?'

As if on cue, a hand-linked teenage couple paused before them in open, sympathetic curiosity. Almost at once they were joined by a flaxen-haired boy, a small, dark man with a camera, another teenage girl.

'You only have to tell me,' Taffy pointed out, shouting as quietly as possible, 'why you weren't hungry. Was it the same reason I wasn't?'

'I could always——' he gazed over the heads of their ever-growing audience, away in the direction he had been steering her '—go on by myself, and leave you here.'

That set her moving at once, with an anxious upwards and sideways glance. Had he noticed how well his threat had worked? The great head tilted for a moment, iron-and-amber eyes meeting hers with a spark which made her look quickly away. Surely he hadn't guessed how her parents had cured her six-year-old tempers when she had them in public?

'Not that I'd have minded if you'd walked away and left me,' she shouted up at him. 'It's just that I've decided this isn't the time, or the place.'

'For what, dormouse?'

And to that she had no answer. She couldn't even say 'for discussing personal affairs', because she wasn't sure they had been. People lost their appetites for all sorts of reasons.

'For talking, I suppose,' she said at last, aware of how vague and weak it sounded.

'Very wise.' He lengthened his stride, so that she had to skip a little to keep up.

'I—er—I am trying, you know,' she shouted, letting him turn her aside so that a family party could stay together.

'Very.' It really wasn't fair the way his big voice got through the surrounding noise so easily.

'You can wisecrack, but I mean it,' she insisted, skipping at his side. 'From now on, I'm going to be really dignified and grown-up... what's that?'

'I was wondering when you'd ask.' He talked just as easily through the new set of noises. 'It's the Shepherd's March.'

'Whee!' She shot ahead of him on dancing feet.

It was impossible not to dance to this music. The drums and silver wind-instruments drove the tune into your mind so that you just had to jig up and down in rhythm, like this little girl beside you...

Taffy managed to still herself before Paul caught up with her. It would never have done for him to see her and the little girl acting as if they were the same age.

'Do the sheep always carry the Luxembourg flag on their backs?' she asked, grave as visiting royalty.

'They carry the Luxembourg colours, anyway,' he confirmed, indicating a half-grown lamb trotting by with a red, white and blue ribbon round its neck.

'I like those blue smocks and red and white necker-chiefs.' She craned out to follow the progress of a cheerful, straw-hatted shepherd. 'I see the bandsmen have them, too.'

'Nowadays it's a form of traditional costume,' he told her. 'But I suppose it comes from what was practical for running a farm. Luxembourgers are all farmers at heart.'

'Where does the march go from here?' she asked when the last fleecy rump was disappearing down the road.

He shrugged. 'Want to follow, and find out?'

'Yes, please!'

'You could be a Luxembourger yourself,' he laughed, taking her hand as they set off. 'You just love a parade.'

Hand-in-hand they followed sheep and shepherds and band, down steep paths, under archways, over bridges, ever deeper into the heart of the old city.

'How cool this still is,' she commented, glad to linger in a narrow cobbled street where the music beat back from high, ancient buildings.

'It always is, down here.' His words grew clearer as the music died away ahead. 'We've the river Alzette one side of us, and the river Pétrusse the other.'

'Luxembourg of the thousand bridges,' she murmured, happy to linger with her hand in his in the suddenly-quiet street. 'The meeting-place of the nations, the stone history of Europe...what is it?' as she felt his sudden stillness.

'I'm thirsty, dormouse.' He had stopped walking and turned to face her, the iron and amber eyes holding hers. 'Are you?'

'Very.' Yet she had the strangest idea that this wasn't about thirst. 'Perhaps we could go back to that last café?'

'Perhaps we could go back, yes.' The arched eyebrows had drawn together over the jutting nose, the dark and bright eyes stared into her and saw she knew not what. 'But not there.'

She waited, conscious of some momentous decision which involved her, though she didn't understand how. She wanted to ask, 'Then where?' but held back in case the words, however soft, should add to this judgement he was making of her, and tip it the wrong way.

Pigeons fluttered overhead. Inside one of the houses a child called, and a woman answered. Somewhere on the edge of hearing, water lapped, and the band threaded its way in and out of the distance.

'*Moyen, Monsieur Seyler. Mademoiselle.*'

Taffy jumped. This Luxembourg greeting, which meant 'Good morning', was used at any time of day, but she wasn't prepared for it here. An old woman in Sunday best nodded at them both, and strolled on with a weary contentment that suggested a newly finished expedition with grandchildren.

'*Moyen, Madame Thill,*' Paul had already answered.

How on earth did he come to know someone so unexpected? Taffy longed to ask, but bit down on the question and refused to let it out.

Perhaps it showed in her eyes, though. At any rate, he seemed to feel it needed some kind of answer.

'Everybody knows everybody, in Luxembourg.'

'I suppose so.' And she smiled, and returned her hand to his. 'Where are we going?'

'I hadn't quite decided.'

He raised her hand and stared down at it, a little ringless paw with its palm resting against his. Then he put his own over it, holding it safe.

'Now I have.'

The old woman was well ahead of them down the street. Paul led Taffy in the same direction, and round a corner, and another, following at a distance as in some leisurely Sunday-afternoon game, until their quarry disappeared into a doorway. He halted Taffy in the shallow-recessed doorway of the next house.

'This is why I know Madame Thill. We're neighbours.'

Taffy blinked, and stood back to look. 'You live *here*?'

The three-storey house was painted with the gentlest of stone colours, with white round the windows. The whole frontage was only wide enough for one window, and for a door with engraved glass panels backed by a curved pattern of wrought-iron.

'It just...just doesn't look big enough...' Taffy stammered, completely bewildered. 'You said you'd moved out of that flat above mine into something bigger...'

'No.' He unlocked the door. 'Into something I liked better, I said.'

'But I was sure it would be...you know...a pent-house, perhaps, with views of the city...'

'This has its views. You'll see.'

Was he watching her? No, he hardly could in this tiny, dark hall, strangely cluttered with shapes you couldn't make out after the brightness outside. Yet still she had that feeling of being tested, of her every move and expression being measured against some secret standard she could easily fail. She realised with a pang that she desperately wanted not to fail it.

'Stand still,' he ordered. 'I'll put on the light.'

She obeyed. Little fountains of light sprang up all round them, and Taffy caught her breath.

'It doesn't feel too closed-in?' But already he sounded easier. 'It doesn't crowd you?'

'No.' All thoughts of self forgotten, she put up a hand in a gesture both confident and entreating. 'Just let me look.'

The open spiral staircase had wooden treads of a dark honey colour. The rest of it was wrought iron, a paradise of iron leaves and flowers and fruit with here a lily edged in silver, there a peach in gold, rioting up through three storeys. Down here in the hall the paradise spread all round the walls, fronds and leaves and branches and blossom parting only for those little bright fountains of light, each placed to set off a different wood-carved group of birds or small animals.

'It's like the beginning of the world.' She touched the textured wings of a pair of doves, courting among gold-glinting wrought-iron apples, and found below them a single coat-hook. 'Fancy hanging your coat in all this!'

He smiled. 'You sound like Joseph. The sculptor,' he added to her enquiring glance. 'He made so much trouble over that coat-peg, I had to let him off giving me an umbrella-stand.'

'I should think so.' She glanced down at the doe grazing with her fawn by the front door. 'Imagine messing these two about with umbrellas.'

He laughed, and slung his jacket on the dove-hook. She watched its dark smoothness settle among the foliage, and had a sudden, uneasy vision of a predator in paradise.

And there's only one kind of predator that sheds its skin, she found herself thinking. The one whose form Lucifer took when he went mischief-making...

But what nonsense, she decided as his tie followed his jacket to the peg and he rolled up his sleeves. No serpent ever had such shoulders, such arms, such a grand, commanding head. And that resonant voice was as far as you could get from the hiss of a serpent.

'Come and see the rest.'

'I haven't finished looking at this yet.' She noticed a squirrel harvesting one of the apples, an owl peering from a frame of iron leaves, a whole family of sparrows. 'Who is this Joseph? Should I have heard of him?'

'Not yet perhaps—this was his first big commission. Don't you want something to drink?'

'Yes, please.' She really was thirsty. '*Citron pressé*?'

'There's lemon, ice and water. You can fix it.'

And she did, in the tiny Delft-tiled kitchen which could only have belonged to a man. She managed to make their lemonade on the draining-board, but the two sharply fragrant halves of squeezed lemon had to stay there; he didn't have a waste-bin. The cupboards held only bottles, and, try as she would, she couldn't locate a stove of any kind.

'Don't you cook at all?' she asked, hunting for a tray.

He produced one, put two glasses on it, and held it to take her jug. 'Never. I eat out, or I have food sent in.' He balanced the tray with utmost care, far more care than it needed. 'Let's go in the living-room.'

But Taffy couldn't. She followed him as far as its door and there she stayed, breathless in the cool, dancing daylight while he set the tray on an inlaid table.

'You really live here?'

'More than that.' He straightened, and let his eyes meet hers full on. 'This is where I really live.'

Still she hesitated. 'And I can really come in?'

'With all my heart, Taffy.'

And so at last she allowed herself to pace the glimmering floorboards. The crystal chandelier dazzled overhead, and below it a bewildering array of objects gave back each its own version of the soothing, shifting gleams you could only have near running water.

'The Alzette,' he murmured, joining her at the window. 'This is one of the oldest parts of the town. Craftsmen used to live here—they needed the river for——'

'Don't talk.' She held up that confident hand, absorbed by the sunlit images in the water, old houses and churches and battlements and bridges forever forming and re-forming against the bright, fractured sky.

She didn't think she could ever get enough of it, but there was so much to see inside as well. Right here next to the window stood a richly curved walnut cupboard, and over there a Trémont panther leapt from its black pedestal, and on the wall a naked Cranach Venus threaded jewels into her hair, and here another picture, modern, showed a little black girl holding a white lamb, and still there was more, more, more.

'It's just you, isn't it?' she breathed at last. 'Everything here's yours, and yours only.'

'Mine and thrice-tested.'

The deep tones had a new note she had never heard before. Could it be triumph? Tenderness? Both? She tried to figure it out as he led her to the wooden settle by the open brick fireplace, then abandoned thought for the pleasure of the tall etched-glass jug cool in her hands. She poured iced lemonade into each etched-glass tumbler, drained her own in a single long draught, and set down her empty glass.

'What did you mean by thrice-tested?'

He tasted his lemonade as if it were wine, one thoughtful sip well swallowed before he answered. 'For a start, I haunt studios, exhibitions, art galleries.'

She nodded eagerly. She loved the visual arts too, though she could seldom afford to buy.

'When I find a piece I like, I visit it again and again, until it becomes a friend.'

Taffy sighed. How often she had done the same thing.

'What I buy, I keep first in the office. If I go on liking it, I take it to the vineyard...'

'Vineyard?' The words Caves Seyler flashed into her mind, the name of one of the Moselle wine-growers. 'Are you that Seyler, then?'

'I'm of that family, yes. A lot of my *objets* I leave there, but sometimes...'

He broke off, and attended once more to his lemonade. Taffy waited, but he would not be hurried.

'Sometimes,' he went on at last, 'there's a piece I want just for me.' He let his gaze travel from the pliant allure of the naked Venus to the fierce innocence of the little black girl. 'When I'm convinced of that, I bring it here.'

And there it was once more in the air between them, that feeling of decision, of judgement, of waiting. Taffy folded her hands on her lap and sat very still, a little afraid, yet certain that this time she must speak.

'That's all very well,' she ventured at last, 'and I can see it works, but...'

She shot him a glance and saw that he was listening intently. So intent was he that he had set aside his unfinished glass, and turned to her the full force of those eyes which were once more dark and mysterious in the water light.

What could she possibly have to say that was worth such attention? And yet thoughts stuck in her mind like burrs, thoughts which must be spoken now and not later, even though, if she spoke them, there might never be a later...

'Don't you ever miss things that way?' she finished in a rush. 'Don't you ever find that by the time you've made your decision it's too late?'

He nodded. 'Until yesterday I'd have said that didn't matter. Now...' He picked up one of her curls and dropped it. 'Now I'm not so sure.'

And here it came again, the rush of her blood to the place where he hadn't quite touched her. Her every separate nerve responded, opened, flooded her with the new awareness he had brought into her life such a short time ago. She felt the tip of her tongue stealing out, and forced it back in dismay. She must say what needed saying, she reminded herself, now or never.

'You're... you're not sure,' she repeated, gradually regaining control of her voice. 'And usually when you're not sure, you do nothing.'

'Usually.' Again that powerful hand approached her, this time touching her cheek lightly with just one finger. 'Not always, though.'

'Not, for instance...' She struggled against new ripples of languor, spreading this time from that tiny place, one fingertip wide, on her cheek. 'Not with your staircase?'

'Mhm.' The small noise of agreement conveyed a world of different, overlapping pleasure, his pleasure in the staircase only the simplest of them. 'I had to commission that. I never really knew how it would work until I'd got it into place.'

'I...I think it's worked brilliantly.' She clung doggedly to her understanding that this wasn't about any of the beautiful things which had already won a place in his house. 'Do you?'

'Mhm.' Again the agreement, the echoing infinity of pleasures. 'Do you want to see where it leads?'

'No!' It came out sharp yet pleading, her hands up to hold him off.

But when he took them in his, and drew her to her feet, she could resist no longer. She felt his lips on each of her fingertips, and in her palm, and on each of her inner wrists where her pulses leapt to meet them. And then they were on hers, drawing her into that whirlpool where no thought could survive, where there were only his arms holding her close, and his body straining towards hers, and a singing infinity of pleasure.

CHAPTER SIX

AT FIRST, it seemed enough.

More than enough. The first time Paul led her up that paradise staircase, Taffy was aware only of his nearness, his hand round hers urging her on, his bare, dark, high-arched feet ahead of hers on the dark-honey treads.

'Whatever became of our shoes?' she murmured.

'I don't know.' He reached the first landing, and turned as she came up level with him so that she stepped from the last tread into his arms. 'I remember taking yours off, and kissing your feet...'

And now he kissed her mouth. She inhaled his wild-thyme fragrance, and offered her tongue to his, and felt his hands on her waist over the loose lime-green dress, and exulted in the curve of her hips because they so clearly pleased him.

Then somehow they were in another room, a cool, bare room furnished with nothing but water lights, water shadows. No, there was something else, a great double bed with a headboard huge as a dark old rock, and linen fresh and inviting as a breeze off the river. Taffy paused before it, trembling, newly reluctant, talking to put off the moment.

'How on earth did you get this in here?'

'In bits.' He lifted her curls, and kissed the back of her neck. 'They assembled it up here.'

'Even then...' She closed her eyes against the next wave of longing, and endured it, and kept her feet. 'Even in bits, you couldn't get it up that staircase without damaging...'

'It was before I got that. But anyway——' his fingers played along her spine, exquisitely sliding and stroking '—the staircase dismantles too, so Joseph can take it to display with his collected work.'

'Goodness!' She resisted those hot, gentle fingers, which would melt her spine if she let them. 'You allow that?'

'I had to promise, or he wouldn't have accepted the job.'

'And you promised?'

'I needed him.'

'Lucky Joseph,' Taffy commented wistfully.

What an example of how to conduct your affairs! If only she had done the same, refused to begin until she had stated her terms, instead of rushing in like a fool...

But what was the use of wishing? Paul had needed the artist for his unique talent. She was just a woman like any other, and no woman would ever impose her own terms on this man. Not even Annette Warren had managed that, Taffy reminded herself.

Yet still she resisted. 'I can't believe your Joseph actually comes and takes all that ironwork away.' She felt his breath warm in her ear, and clung to her detached, rational, inconsequential thoughts. 'The treads must look naked.'

'They might, I suppose.' He had started kissing the back of her shoulder, now also mysteriously naked. 'But he takes those too, as an intrinsic part of the work.'

'What?' She turned in disbelief. 'How on earth do you manage without a staircase...?'

She broke off in dismay. Her body had turned as it meant to, but her dress and bra only slithered free and dropped to her waist, leaving her blinking down at her own exuberant, demanding breasts. So that was what he'd been doing at her back, loosening and unfastening in that mysterious way he had.

He completed what he had begun. A little push, a little tug, a little further opening of a zip, and her dress slid to the floor, taking the rest of her clothes with it.

'No!' She stiffened her hands before her, refusing his embrace, refusing even the sensual pleasure of that great, warm chest under her longing fingertips. 'Not till...'

She trailed off, unable to say it. Not till you need me the way you needed the artist who made that staircase, she wanted to say, but could not. Not till we both know that I'm the only person in the world who can give you what you want...

'What is it, dormouse?' Impatiently he eyed the fullness of her breasts, pushed together between her distance-keeping arms.

'Not till...'

But it was no use, she couldn't go on. She had to let him swing her off her feet, had to nestle to the solid warmth of his shoulder, and rub her cheek on the dear, private disorder of his hair, and revel in the strength which carried her so lightly over the bare floorboards to the cool, huge island of the bed.

'So what's worrying you?' He sat by her, eyes devouring her body. 'You know what you make me think of? Pearls under water. I've never seen pearls under water, but this——' he cupped a hand over one of her breasts '—is how they must look. All right, all right!' He smiled at its urgent response to his palm, and stood up. 'All in good time.'

She lay where he had set her on the cool duvet, watching his own deft undressing. First the shirt dropped from the wide shoulders, and lay in a heap where it fell on the sand-coloured floorboards. The trousers followed, and he padded away on muscled, purposeful legs into the glimmering river shadows at the foot of the bed.

How healthy his skin was. It shone like the coat of a thoroughbred horse, taking and giving back the dancing light in ever-changing patterns. A dusting of hair darkened his forearms, but the glowing muscles of his upper arms each had its own highlight, and to each of their tiniest movements the muscles of his back responded and re-formed in perfect harmony on either side of the long furrow of his spine.

So absorbed was Taffy in that superbly proportioned back, it took her a moment to realise why he had turned it. When she did, a little sadness tugged at her. He was doing what was right, she knew he was, and yet, and yet... She found herself speaking aloud, catching at any random thought to distract herself.

'I'm an experienced woman now, aren't I?'

The muscled highlights formed a new pattern, turning his head to show eyes dark with tender mockery. 'You are?'

'Well, aren't I?' She bridled. 'Experienced enough to know that we mustn't risk...'

Once more, she had to stop. Her defence against her own inner desires had been too frail; already it lay shattered by her own careless, unspoken word. She knew now that somewhere deep down, deeper than words or thought or reason, she wanted that risk she hadn't been able to name. Whatever the cost, a deep, primeval, unsuspected part of her longed to bear his child.

'No, we mustn't.'

He was answering her unfinished comment about risk, she realised with a start. The same answer would have done for this new-discovered longing within her, but he must never know about that. Her body was his, she had given it last night, a lifetime ago, in heedless, impulsive haste. But he wouldn't get this new understanding which was just beginning to grow within her. That was hers, all she had left, and she would protect it any way she could...

'What on earth's the matter with you, dormouse?' He rose and padded towards her, dark and powerful as a river-god in the shimmering river light. 'I've said it twice now, and still you haven't answered.'

'What?' She blinked helplessly up at him. 'What haven't I answered?'

'Never mind.' It came out a low growl of desire as he sank to her side. 'It'll keep...'

The words trailed off, buried in her breasts. She gasped, and treasured his ruffled hair, and let him start her on the slow river-journey of pleasure. Presently his lips left her breasts to possess the rest of her, shoulders and arms and sides, waist and hips and thighs, until she tossed away from him in an ecstasy of longing.

'It's not fair, Paul. I must touch you...'

'Touch,' he growled.

And she did, with hands and lips and tongue. Her lips preferred the smooth hollows above and below his shoulder-blades, her tongue the intriguing folds of his navel, but her hands loved every part of him as much as the next.

Or perhaps it was his hair they liked best? Her stroking fingers explored once more the fine, thick swaths on his head, then followed one strong eyebrow from where it started at the side of his nose to where it finished at his high, square temple. That led naturally to the barely subdued stubble of his jaw, where a beard would come the minute it was let, and from there it was only the shortest leap to the new texture, soft and rough together, of the sprinkled hair on his chest.

And it never really stopped, that body-hair. It almost did, but you could feel here how it went on down, the finest line, until here, where it broadened and strengthened and curled, the better to support...

'Careful!' He grabbed her wrist.

'Yes, of course.' She flounced her own riotous hair over her face. 'We always have to be careful, don't we?'

'What's the matter?' His voice sharpened, almost surfacing from the river-depths of pleasure.

'The staircase,' she murmured incoherently. 'How do you manage when you lose your paradise staircase?'

'I have to find some other way to paradise. This one, for instance.'

'Oh!' she gasped, astonished. 'Oh, my goodness!'

'Is it good this time, dormouse?' he asked, lips against her cheek.

'It's marvellous...'

She struggled for words to express the satisfaction, the completeness of possessing him within her. But he advanced and she had to contain, he thrust and she had to answer with thrusts of her own. Slowly at first and then ever faster they drove together through leaping rapids of sensation, surge upon surge, to the inner headwaters of desire. Then came the everywhere and nowhere of desire's end, where you spun like a planet, drifted like thistledown, and found yourself at last returned to where you started, in your lover's arms.

Because he was her lover now. She did at least have that. He might never father her children, he might never be her husband, but she mustn't let what she couldn't have spoil what she had. He was hers here and now. It would have to be enough.

And it almost was. The agreeable indolence of afterlove was in its own way almost as sweet as love itself. She lay with her head on his shoulder, and heard his

voice rumbling in his chest as he told her of his latest
business venture, which strangely had something to do
with ceramics, and something to do with the steel in-
dustry. She never did understand the connection, and
was too lazy to care.

'What's a wine-grower doing in ceramics anyway?' she
asked. 'Let alone owning apartment-blocks...'

'Only one apartment block,' he corrected her, as if
that were a very modest share, and stroked her hair. 'One
thing leads to another. I turned out to be good at making
money.'

She set her lips to his wrist, enjoying first its hair-
roughened, sinewy strength, and then the vulnerable flesh
of its inner side. 'So who looks after the vineyard?'

'It does all right.' But a sigh lifted the deep chest, as
if the world and its demands were edging back. 'I'll have
to settle down there soon, though.'

She raised her head, catching some of his unease. 'Do
you mean you'll have to take over the wine business?'

'That, too, but not specially. No, it's just time I settled
down. I'll be thirty next birthday...don't do that.'

'Why not?' she asked, thrilled at the change she could
bring about with one exploring hand. 'You seem to like
it.'

'Hussy!'

He grabbed the hand, and nipped the cushion of its
thumb in white, even teeth. Then he set it away from
him on the pillow, and slid his shoulder from under her
head.

'I like it a lot, dormouse.' But he was sitting up and
swinging his feet to the floor, not looking at her. 'Not
now, though. I haven't time.'

How cold it felt to be alone again, and how lonely.
He had put her aside so gently, and yet now she felt
deserted, left behind, a mere incident in his busy life.

She lay watching his magnificent uncoiling, and thought of a river-god who had taken his pleasure with a mortal. It was over, and he was ready to return to his own domain. What else did she expect?

'Where have you got to go, then?' Her own voice sounded thin and sour in her ears. 'Or shouldn't I ask?'

He turned to look down at her over that wide, muscled, lost shoulder. 'We need to eat——'

'We?' she interrupted, reviving.

'I'm hungry, after all that exercise.' His eyes caressed her naked length. 'Aren't you?'

She was out of the bed before she knew it, the floorboards cool under her feet. 'We're to eat together?'

'I begin to see the gymnast in you, dormouse.' He was laughing at her again. 'You jump like a jack-in-the-box.'

'I am hungry, now that I think of it,' she told him with dignity. 'Can I have a shower first?'

'Only if you share it with me.'

'That's blackmail . . .' She stopped, intrigued. 'Is your shower big enough for two?'

'Come and see.'

So that was what he had up here on the top floor. The white door had an enamel plaque on the outside, showing a modest, high-stomached medieval lady with tight-bound hair and flowing green gown. On the other side of the door the lady had become a mermaid, with un-bound, gold-glinting hair curling to her green and gold tail.

'It's Melusine,' Taffy exclaimed, enchanted to recognise the wife of the founder of Luxembourg. 'Was this done by another of your artist friends?'

He nodded. 'I'm glad Melusine the mermaid's on the inside, though. I like her much better than Melusine the chatelaine.'

'Well, you would, wouldn't you?'

Of course he would prefer the river-sprite, the creature from his own other world away from the little affairs of mortals. When he crossed the marble floor to the un-curtained shower, she followed with a sense of chill, until she reached the shining taps and levers of the huge sunken bath.

'No, you can't play with the Jacuzzi.' Paul put his hands on her waist and drew her away. 'You get a shower or nothing.'

'Spoilsport!' She resisted at first, but on second thoughts turned and stole her arms round his neck. 'I've always wanted to make love in a Jacuzzi,' she insinuated close to his ear.

His flesh sprang against her, and she surged lovingly, exultantly towards it. She might be ordinary, a nobody, a mere incident in his life, but this power she did have.

'What a lot I'm finding out about you, Paul Seyler.'

'And there's more.' He disentangled himself ruth-lessly, made for the shower, and fiddled with its controls.

'You can't hide from me over there.' She skipped up and down in front of him, taunting him with her jiggling breasts. 'I can still see how you——'

She finished with an indignant squeal. The cold spray had hit her right in the midriff, almost shocking the breath from her. She wrapped her arms round herself and turned her back, but the icy jet went on and on, up and down her spine until she felt her blood racing and her skin glowing.

'Like the inside of a sea-shell,' she heard him murmur, and the spray left her.

When she dared to open her eyes and look, he had hooked the nozzle back in place. Its shrivelling-cold water poured down on himself only as he squeezed cream from a tube into his cupped hand, then rubbed it to a foam which filled the wet air with the scent of wild thyme.

'Come on in.' He held both lathered hands out to her.

'No!' She shivered at the stray drops running down her skin. 'Not till you've turned on the hot... keep away from me!'

She retreated, but one of his long strides was more than enough for him to grab her arms. His hot-cold, soap-slippery hands, clamping to keep their hold, dug cruelly into her flesh.

'You beast! Let go!' She resisted every inch, but couldn't stop him dragging her under the stream of cold water. 'Ooooh!' She flinched and wriggled and revelled. 'It's horrible! You're a tyrant, a monster, a bully...'

'Maybe.' He pulled her close, wrapped her in his own shining, cool-surfaced warmth, and ran his hands down her back. 'But I'll soon be a clean bully, and then a well-fed one.'

The hair on his chest sparkled with scattered drops. She pressed against it, loving the way it rasped her skin but refusing to forgive him.

'You've wet all my hair.'

'We might as well wash it, then. Turn around.'

She obeyed, sniffing up the rich thyme scent of the shampoo he was squeezing into her hair. His strong fingers worked it into a lather, and then something delightful happened. The water suddenly ran at exactly the right temperature.

A blissful languor stole over her. The mirrored wall opposite showed her shining-pale, hair piled stiff as a powdered wig. Paul appeared as a darker, harder frame to her paleness, his long muscles flexing in the filtered light as he moved with the leisure of accustomed command.

He left her hair and stroked the lather downwards. She felt those hard, gentle hands working it into her shoulder-blades and spine and hips, then they swooped

and skimmed and settled on the backs of her thighs.
Lovingly they circled and polished, ever downwards,
knees, calves, heels, insteps...

She turned to him with mock-innocence. 'You've
missed a lot of bits out.'

'Those,' he told her severely, 'you can do for yourself.'

'No, I'm going to do you now.' She took the shampoo
from where he had put it on a soap-dish. 'Kneel down.'

'Watch it, dormouse.' He clearly didn't intend to obey.
'However appetising you are, I swear I won't eat you
instead of supper.' He put out a hand to take the tube
from her. 'I'll wash myself.'

'No, you won't.' She held the shampoo behind her.
'If you won't kneel, bend so I can wash your hair.'

He sighed. 'Be quick, then.'

He bent his knees uncomfortably, bringing his head
below the level of hers. It was, she discovered, an ideal
position for her to trail her breasts against his cheek...

'Stop that!' He turned his face away.

'Don't you want me any more?' she asked, well able
to see why the question was absurd.

'I want my supper, you little pest.' He straightened,
and made to seize the shampoo.

'No, no, I'll be good.' She turned to keep it from him,
hurriedly squeezing a white blob into her palm. 'Let me!'

Grumbling, he bent again, and she delighted in the
pliancy of his hair under the soap and water. Seeing there
was so much lather to spare, she used it up as he had
for her, working it slowly downwards. When he had
straightened in relief and turned away from her, she
soaped his back, underarms, legs and heels.

'Now your front,' she said gleefully.

'You're taking a hell of a time.'

'There's a lot of you. Turn round.'

But he wouldn't. He simply picked up a tablet of thyme-scented soap, and went ahead and washed himself as he'd always intended. Taffy took her revenge by skipping away and coming back on the other side of him, to stare unashamedly. The hot water ran over him in shining streams, which parted in the most fascinating place. What would happen if she knelt like this, and raised her breasts like this, as a kind of double cushion...

What happened was that he put his hands under her armpits, hauled her upright, and held her head direct under the jet which he had switched back to cold.

'Aaow!' she squeaked. 'Why did you do that?'

'As if you didn't know.' He kept her under the icy stream, pushing his fingers through her hair to rinse off the soap. 'Now——' he released her at last '—go and dry yourself.'

'Yes, Paul.'

She kissed his shoulder, and dripped over the marble tiles to the towel-rail. It only held two towels, she discovered, a big one and a smaller, but both were deep and welcoming.

'It still seems an awful pity,' she commented when he had joined her and she had handed him the bigger towel.

'It's one thing or the other.' He dried himself briskly, understanding exactly what she had meant. 'Come on, we haven't got long.'

'Haven't we?' She trailed after him, down between the silver-edged iron lilies and grapes, the gold-edged iron peaches and roses. 'What have you got to do that's so urgent?'

He had disappeared through another, unexplored door. She peered in, and found it led to a room the same size as the kitchen downstairs, severe white like the bedroom but with a mirrored end wall like the bathroom, and one of the lengthways walls made up entirely of dark-glowing, polished sliding doors.

He swished one of the doors along its groove. 'I've got to be up at...' He broke off, threw her a glance, and vanished into the deep cupboard. 'Go and get your clothes on,' his voice came muffled from within it. 'I really haven't long.'

'All right.' She trailed into the bedroom where the river light had softened to evening, and took up her battered clothes. 'You won't be too formal, will you, Paul?' she called as she put them on. 'The *Scheuberfouer* was a bit hard on this dress.'

'And not only the *Scheuberfouer*,' the muffled voice responded.

She sighed at how far away he sounded. Already he'd left her, following some plan he didn't want to speak of into some place she was determined not to ask about. His gold watch lay by the window, waiting for him to put it on and start them both moving through time on their separate tracks, away from each other into their separate futures.

'Hm.' He was with her and surveying her crumpled lime-green cotton. 'I do see what you mean.'

'You look nice.' She took in his light trousers and casual jacket. 'If I could go home and change...'

'No time.' He fastened on the beautiful, hateful watch as if it were a friend. 'Don't worry, it's a very quiet place where we're going.'

The very quiet place turned out to have a comfortable number of customers. However, the young *patron* appeared at once from some opening in the panelling, and made his way through the blue and white tablecloths and shaded lamps with his hand held out to Paul in greeting. Introduced to Taffy in English as Monsieur Faber, he gave her a courteous bow which didn't quite conceal a lively curiosity, and led them to a corner table shielded by plants.

'Not that you need to hide, even in that dress.' Paul ran an appreciative eye over Taffy as he took his place opposite her. 'Love suits you.'

She felt herself blushing, and stared unseeing at her copy of the big leather-bound menu. Did their recent lovemaking stand out so very clearly? Was that why the young restaurateur had been so interested in her? Had he guessed?

'Do you think they all know?' she asked, longing to be reassured.

'Who's "they"?' He was turning the pages of his own menu in the manner of one who knew his way through it. 'And what might they know?'

'What we've been doing,' she snapped. 'How can you be so interested in food, at a time like this?'

'How can you not be?' He raised those thick, devil's eyebrows. 'I'm sure nobody gives a damn what we've been doing.'

'I bet they can guess.' She peered through the greenery at the busy room. 'I'm glad this table was free.'

'It always is.' He turned another page, making his choice. 'The Fabers save it for me.'

So easily could your peace be shattered. She was suddenly, crushingly aware of how little she knew of him and his life. She could picture him eating here with one beautiful woman after another, Annette Warren only the latest of them . . .

But no, she told herself with a deep sense of shock. It isn't Annette who's his latest affair, it's me.

'I'm having the *rôti de veau aux cèpes*,' he announced, his matter-of-fact tone completely at odds with this new, boiling misery inside her. 'Are you hungry enough for that, dormouse?'

Taffy, far from being hungry enough for roast veal with mushrooms, had stopped being hungry at all. She shook her head to one after another of his suggestions, until he put down the menu with quizzical patience.

'So what are you having?'

She looked again through the fronds and leaves. The long central table held fruit and flowers, and cartwheels of cake, and bottles of wine, and a huge round tray of cheeses.

'A piece of Camembert,' she decided at last.

He frowned. 'That won't keep you going for long.'

'It will. I like Camembert.'

He shrugged, and summoned the waiter. While they discussed the order Taffy sat with bowed head, determined not to glance up at either man, hating the thought of how she must seem, sitting here as Paul Seyler's latest.

'Taffy.' Paul had poured white wine into her glass, and returned the bottle to its basket cradle. 'What's the matter?'

'Nothing.' She put out a hand for her glass, and recoiled in shock when he slapped it away.

'Wait till the food comes,' he admonished. 'You don't drink Pinot Gris on an empty stomach; it isn't fair to the wine.'

'And we must be fair to the wine, mustn't we?' she responded savagely. 'That matters a lot more than being fair to the women you get mixed up with.'

'What the hell are you on about?' A frown pulled the arched brows together. 'How did women get into this?'

'I suppose you'd prefer not to talk about the others you've brought here.' She stared down at the blue-checked cloth to shut out those dark, penetrating eyes. 'Same as you won't talk about me with the next one.'

When he didn't answer, she stole another glance at him. His frown had gone, replaced by that rock-hewn, controlled mask of anger she found so hard to face. She stared down again, hearing the small noises of the restaurant. A plate rattled, wine gurgled into a glass, some lucky woman laughed. .

'I wonder if it's brought on by lovemaking?' he began at last with menacing lightness. 'This is the second time you've turned poisonous——'

'Poisonous!' Her head jerked up. 'How dare you——?'

'—and this time you're spoiling a good supper.'

'You see,' she exclaimed, for herself as much as for him. 'That's the kind of man you are, Paul Seyler, a materialist through and through...'

'These other women I'm supposed to bring here.' The deep voice easily rode hers. 'I seldom eat at home, remember? This is where I have most of my meals.' The hard mouth closed, then rapped out one word more. 'Alone.'

Alone. She looked across at the dark, deep eyes, the carved prow of a nose, the uncompromising mouth, and knew he was telling the truth. He wasn't speaking to comfort, far from it. Quite simply, he scorned lying.

'So you don't bring women here,' she muttered, a little ashamed yet still obscurely angry. 'But there've been plenty of them, haven't there?'

'That——' he glanced down at his hateful watch '—is none of your business.'

'You see?' she exclaimed again helplessly. 'You call what we just did *lovemaking*, yet you shut me out of your life...'

'Only from what happened before we ever met.'

'And from what's about to happen after we part,' she insisted, maddened by his awareness of time passing when she so wanted it to stand still. 'After we've eaten, when you rush off without me to wherever it is...'

'So that's it.'

He set his hands palm down on the table. They seemed so relaxed and quiet, those hands, that she dared to look again at his face. Sure enough, the rock-hewn anger had gone, replaced by a thoughtfulness which curled the hard mouth into new lines and kept the dark eyes relentlessly on hers. She tried to drag her own glance away but couldn't; it had to stay tangled with his while that scalpel mind laid bare thoughts she hadn't known she was thinking.

'If you wanted to know where I'm going,' he said at last, 'why didn't you ask me?'

'A p-person...' As if her own voice had broken his hold on her, she faced him with fresh courage. 'A person has her pride.'

'And her poison.' But he wasn't seeking to wound now, only to point an argument. 'Instead of bringing it out in the open, dormouse, you've let it go bad inside you.'

Yet even now he was glancing once more at that wretched watch. She stared across at it, and then back to his face, with something like despair.

'You still aren't telling me.'

'I didn't intend to,' he admitted, 'for all sorts of reasons. But seeing it upsets you so much...' Another pause, unknown factors being weighed and balanced behind those perceptive eyes. 'I suppose I'd better,' he went on at last. 'I'm going to see...' He stopped, glanced round the ever more crowded restaurant, and found another way of putting it. 'I'm due back at the hospital.'

'Hospital?' she repeated, relieved and at once ready to sympathise. 'Who do you know who's in...?' She stopped, light dawning and with it guilt. 'Claudia!'

'Not so loud!' He glanced towards the nearest table of peaceful diners. 'She doesn't want it known where

she is. Luckily I booked her in under her real
name——'

'And I,' Taffy cut in, her hatred suddenly turned on
herself, 'forgot all about her. Come back at noon, they
said, and I didn't even remember.'

'That's just as well.' The deep voice was suddenly
gentle. 'The best thing would be if you kept on
forgetting.'

Taffy felt worse than ever as she remembered the
sudden closeness she had felt with Claudia, the affection
for a fellow being who needed her help. 'At least tell me
how she is.'

'Getting on well enough.' But those shutters had come
down behind the dark eyes, making the answer so general
as to be meaningless. 'She'll have to be careful, though.'

'I bet. You can't mess about with an ulcer.'

'An . . .' He glanced at her sharply, then came to some
decision behind those shuttered eyes. 'No. No, you can't.'

'There's no hope——' Taffy felt small, selfish, un-
deserving, yet had to put in her plea '—of her seeing me
now?'

'None.' He turned almost in relief as Monsieur Faber
himself appeared at their table bearing silver dishes.
'She's not seeing anybody.'

Taffy stared down at her wedge of Camembert, not
wanting it. 'She's seeing you.'

'And only me.'

He thanked Monsieur Faber, and turned his attention
to his meal like a door closing.

CHAPTER SEVEN

AND that was how it had to stay. Left alone with Taffy at their table, Paul ate purposefully and for a while parried all her questions. He finally reacted only when she begged to be told Claudia's real name.

'Don't be silly, dormouse. That isn't mine to tell.'

'But you just said you gave it at the hospital.'

'Nobody there recognises her.' He put his knife and fork together with an air of finality. 'To them, she's just a woman needing help.'

'That's exactly what she is to me,' Taffy pointed out, more and more frustrated. 'I could at least send flowers or something, if I knew who to send them to.'

'Forget it.'

He signalled a passing waiter. The man removed his plate, nodded to the request for a bill, and departed with just one quick, inquisitive glance at Taffy.

'No flowers, no enquiries, nothing,' Paul went on when they were alone once more. 'She doesn't want anything except——'

'Except you?' Taffy cut in, and choked down another sawdust mouthful of cheese.

Would he deny it? Please, please let him deny it. Best of all let him laugh at the idea, and dismiss it, and somehow prove that this bond between him and a glamorous, fascinating older woman couldn't possibly ever have existed.

But he didn't. Instead he silently held her eyes, his own hooded and unreadable. Which would be strongest in them now, she wondered, the iron or the amber? You needed the clear light of day to answer such questions, not this shaded table-lamp.

'Except you,' she repeated, forcing it out. 'It's you she wants, isn't it?'

He bunched his blue and white napkin and dumped it on the table with a hardly audible sigh. 'If only it were that simple.'

'You'd... you'd like it to be?' She couldn't keep her voice from trembling.

The dark eyes returned to hers. 'I'd like Claudia's affairs to be simpler, yes. Now, dormouse——' he consulted that villainous, unforgiving watch '—finish your cheese, and we'll be off.'

She wanted to throw her plate at him. She wanted at least to jump up and run away, rather than sit tame and still until he was ready to escort her. Only the thought of how well he was known here kept her quietly in her seat, aware of all the eager interest she would fuel with such a scene. She cut off another piece of Camembert and stared down at it, wondering at herself. Was she really enduring this miserable inaction, just to save him from being talked about?

'Right.' He reached across and lifted her plate towards him. 'I'll finish this for you.'

'I never said I couldn't eat it,' she scolded. 'And anyway, it wouldn't have been a crime to leave it.'

'No?' He took the unused knife from his own setting and methodically cut the cheese. 'I hope you're not going to turn out to be one of those women who ill-treat food, dormouse?'

Now why should that make her feel suddenly better? Sitting up straighter, breathing easier, she realised it was because he'd sounded as if meant to find out whether she was that kind of woman or not. He'd spoken as if they had a future together.

'What about the kind of man you're turning out to be?' she demanded. 'The kind who...'

But she had to break off. The kind who keeps secrets, she'd wanted to say, a two-timer. And yet how could he be? Hadn't he advised her only a minute ago to bring her worries out into the open? Hadn't he said that if you didn't they turned poisonous?

'The kind who hates to see good food go to waste,' he put in through a mouthful of cheese. 'And this is really very good...'

'Food again,' she reproached him. 'Can't you ever think of anything else?'

'Lots of other things,' he answered equably. 'For instance, how did you enjoy your Pinot Gris?'

She blinked at her glass, and saw with astonishment that it was empty. 'I ... I don't really remember...'

He shook his head in disapproval. 'You mustn't do that to good wine, dormouse.'

'You see?' She returned with relief to the attack. 'Wine and food, food and wine—and you talk about *me* being fat!'

'What an idea,' he exclaimed in mock horror. 'You're just round enough to be appetising...'

'Appetite again!' She pounced on the word. 'Those appetites of yours'll come home to roost some day, you'll see. Just wait till you're fat as a pumpkin...'

She broke off. For a moment, she realised with surprise, she had actually relaxed, and enjoyed teasing him the way he always did her. But oh, dear, why had she mentioned pumpkins of all things? The mere picture of one in her mind, the swelling fertility of it, reminded her of the pregnancy he'd taken such care to avoid...

'I have my methods for staying thin.' He shot her a swift, private glance. 'Love in the afternoon, for instance.'

She almost asked him how often, and with how many women, but managed not to. 'And like all your pleasures,' she retorted, veiling her pain, 'that one's strictly materialistic.'

'I am what I am, dormouse.' He opened his wallet as Monsieur Faber approached with the bill. 'Take it or leave it.'

And she took it, because she hadn't any choice. The bill paid, he walked her to one of the car parks she found so surprising in the crowded spaces of this endlessly surprising city. There, he put her into the car she had last seen at the hospital, and drove her through the narrow streets to her—his—apartment block.

'Good,' he observed as he opened the street door for her. 'I see the lift's down here.'

'I never use it.'

She meant it as an assertion of independence, but it came out too subdued for that. Going before him into the dim, cool entrance hall, she felt small and weak and ludicrously defenceless. Was this how the prey felt before the predator took it? Yet what had he taken from her that she hadn't freely given? Only her pride, she realised as she nerved herself for the question she must ask.

'Do I...?' She heard the uncertain note in her own voice, and did her best to lighten it. 'Do I get to see you again?'

'What a question.'

He bent to kiss her. Feeling those hard lips brushing her own, she had to put her hand on his shoulder. His fingers closed on her wrist, and he pulled it away to set a kiss in her palm. Then he was gone, with nothing more said about another meeting. When she thought back over that last brief exchange, she realised he hadn't committed himself on that in any way.

Luckily, the next day at work proved to be a busy one. Feeding the computer with new addresses for the Euro-journal, checking over the English-language press handout on road safety, locating the missing paperwork on microchip technology might not be the most stimu-lating tasks, but they did keep her mind off her troubles until the midday break. Only in the cafeteria at the top of the tower building was she suddenly, forcibly re-minded of what she would rather have forgotten.

'Come and sit here,' commanded Kendra Morgan as Taffy passed with her tray. 'I've saved you the window-place.'

'Thanks.' Taffy took the place opposite the older woman, set out her grilled trout and salad, and paused as always to enjoy the European Centre below, and beyond it the old city dropping into blue distance. 'How do you ever manage to take this view for granted?'

Kendra dismissed it with a wave of her hand. 'I hear you were at Faber's yesterday with Paul Seyler. Don't clam up on me, love,' she added, motherly face creased with concern. 'It's you I'm thinking of. He broke Annette's heart, you know.'

Taffy thought of that bright coral heart, and crushed down the comment that it wouldn't break easily. Even in her short time here she had learnt that happily married Kendra loved to fuss over the younger women in the office. As far as Kendra was concerned they were never wrong; she was always on their side against the world.

'I doubt if we'll ever get that far,' Taffy said instead. 'I don't even know if I'm going to see him again.'

'That's exactly how he was with Annette,' Kendra pointed out. 'She never knew where she was with him. She asked her father here specially to meet him——' another colleague approached their table, and was smil-ingly waved away '—but Paul Seyler never returned the compliment,' Kendra finished when they were alone once more.

Taffy dissected her trout. 'What compliment?'

'Why, inviting her to meet his family, of course.'

'He has one, then?' Taffy stared out at the bright, racing summer clouds, and remembered how she had asked Paul if he was connected with the wine-growing Seylers.

'I'm of that family, yes,' he'd answered, and had gone on at once to speak of something else.

'The vineyard's run by his mother, Madame Seyler,' Kendra chatted on. 'But Annette never even saw her, except on one of those guided visits.' Kendra waved vaguely to indicate a public guided tour of the wine-vaults. 'She took it so she could at least get a look at the place.'

'She did that?' Taffy asked, shocked.

'Why shouldn't she? All's fair——'

'I see you're having the *poulet*,' Taffy hurriedly interrupted. 'What's it like?'

And so the day wore on. Taffy's flat, when she let herself into it that evening seemed not only empty, but repulsive. This place wasn't hers, she realised with unbearable clarity, it was Annette Warren's. She wouldn't go on living here, she would give notice at once. She would find out what else was available, straight away if the agency was still open...

But when the telephone book was in her hands, the pages turned automatically to the 'S's. And however much she searched among the Seylers she couldn't find a number, not for his flat here, not for the house by the Alzette. He must be ex-directory, which was just as well because she wouldn't ever have rung him, no, she would not...

'Coming!' her voice soared happily as she rushed to answer her doorbell. 'Oh.' She drooped just as quickly when she opened the door. 'Hello, Nick. You might as well come in, I suppose.'

'You certainly know how to make a guy feel welcome.' Nick lounged into the living-room after her. 'Paul said I had to apologise for yesterday. You know,' impatiently, 'getting you dizzy, and all.'

'Oh. That's all right.' Taffy dismissed it, heart thumping. 'When did he tell you to do that? He's not here in the building, is he?'

'Nah, that was yesterday. It's my belief he's with Claudia now.' Nick dropped into the big chair she couldn't help thinking of as Paul's. 'I rang him at his office, but he won't say which hospital. Actually...' Nick cleared his throat. 'You'd know that, wouldn't you? Seeing you went there.'

'I might, I suppose.' Taffy recalled the late night drive through the unknown streets, and the early morning walk back. 'I'm hopeless on directions, but maybe with a map...' She broke off, shrugging. 'There's no point in racking our brains about it, we can't go there. Claudia doesn't want visitors.'

Nick bridled. 'This isn't visitors, it's *me*. I've bought flowers.'

'She doesn't want those either. No flowers, no enquiries, nothing.'

Taffy was astonished to hear herself echoing so firmly what Paul had told her last night. Yes, and knowing how he'd felt when he'd said it, and understanding why. There must be hundreds of people like Nick, like herself, who would be perfectly confident that Claudia, however much she needed to stay quiet, would be delighted to see them. She recognised with a shock what such people had in common.

We're all so important to ourselves, she thought, we're sure we must be important to everyone else.

And here was Nick, confirming these uncomfortable new ideas with every word he uttered. 'She's specially fond of me, that's why she was going to be in the video,' he pleaded. 'I know she'd see me, if I could only find out where she is.'

'I can't help you,' Taffy announced with new decision, 'but if I could I wouldn't. Things like that aren't mine to tell.'

'Not mine to tell.' Weren't those the words Paul had used when she'd pleaded to know Claudia's real name? Taffy inwardly cringed at the memory. How could she ever have demanded such private information? Of course you didn't give it out to everyone who asked, just because they wanted to know.

The rest of Nick's arguments and persuasions washed over her unheeded. When he gave up and stamped out, she went to the door with him, more aware of his gangly movements and general immaturity than of anything he said. He wasn't just the centre of his own world, he was the only person in it who mattered.

She closed the door on him with relief, and lingered to stare at herself in the hall mirror with renewed shame. Was this how she appeared to others? Was this how they saw her?

'Who am I trying to kid?' She shook her head, determined to learn her lesson well. 'It's Paul I'm thinking of. Is this how *he* sees me?'

Green, he'd called her, and untried, and unseasoned. And how right he'd been. Her own round face stared back at her, green-hazel eyes shallow and untested as they must always have been, though she had never noticed it before.

'No wonder he didn't want to see you again,' she told her tear-blurred reflection. 'No wonder he called you dormouse. The question is, when are you ever going to wake up?'

If he ever came back to her, if she was ever so lucky, she'd stop being a dormouse and start being a real, grown-up woman. And her first step to that, she told herself two hours later, was to accept that he wasn't going to come back at all, and to grow up anyway, simply because it was high time she did.

'All the same,' she told the silent telephone, 'I'll give you just a little longer.'

And a little. And a little. She waited until the late summer light faded, and made it easier than ever to conjure up the man who might have been over there in the big armchair. Then she dragged herself to the too big, solitary bed.

It was surprising how peacefully you slept when you'd given up hope. In the morning, tempted to skip her lonely breakfast, she made herself set it as usual in the dining-alcove off the living-room. She might as well get used to it, and to finding comfort in small things like this delicate china, the first she had ever owned. When the coffee started to gurgle she could almost look forward to drinking it. After all, it was something to have known...whatever it was she had known with Paul Seyler.

'I won't ever marry, of course,' she said aloud over the rushing of her lonely shower. 'The boys all will, and then I can be their children's old spinster auntie.'

And if that seemed too little and too late, well, there was always work. A good secretary could go far, if she kept her mind on it. This grey skirt and white blouse would set exactly the note for that, and, in case anyone thought them too sober, here was a copper-green floaty scarf to knot at her neck.

Thus prepared for her prudent, hard-working, empty future, she took up her purse and basket and key. Only two days ago, she had found this foreign ritual of fetching a fresh roll for breakfast perfectly delightful. Now, well, it was still something. Today she'd buy a croissant, and bother the calories. She could practically smell it already, nose twitching as she opened her front door...

'Aaah!' She jumped back with a small scream. 'What are you doing here?'

'Can't a guy visit?' Paul grinned, demonic with good health in that dark running outfit. 'Especially when he's brought along breakfast.'

Taffy stood in the doorway, still a little shaky. It took some getting used to, this great dark figure materialising before you like your desires made flesh. Or, anyway, like your desires would have been if you'd imagined anything like the olive glow of health over these high cheekbones, the play of biceps revealed by that short-sleeved black T-shirt, the smooth throat rising from its turtleneck...

'Come on, come on!' Every well-exercised muscle meshing with springy ease, he dangled the delicious-smelling paper bags in front of her nose. 'I'm hungry!'

'When are you ever not?'

But she let him in, giving way as she always did. As she always would, she realised, a small note of despair amid her tumult of joy at seeing him again. Whatever he chose to do, with her or without her, she would always give way. This was how it had to be, him leading, her following as she was doing now, back through her own hall, over to her own dining-alcove...

'Hm.' He surveyed her tulip-patterned breakfast-cloth with the single strawberry-patterned place-setting. 'I like this.'

'You do?' She was pleased, but surprised. 'Wouldn't it be better if the crockery matched the cloth?'

'Not for me it wouldn't. I like it uncoordinated. Uncalculated.' He dumped his bags on the table. 'Not like it was when...'

She waited for him to go on, and as he didn't, she said it for him. 'When Annette was here?'

He only nodded towards the single setting. 'I hope you've lots more of this china. We'll need it.'

She moved obediently to fetch it, but couldn't resist a small rebellion. 'You're the one who started talking about her. Even if you didn't get as far as mentioning her name.'

'I admit it, dormouse.'

'You do?' she turned in the doorway, newly surprised. 'I didn't think men ever admitted anything. My brothers...'

'There's only enough coffee here for one cup each. I always have two.'

'I'll buy a bigger filter-outfit,' she exclaimed joyfully.

'No need for that. Come on, where are those plates?' he added, quite unaware of how he had dashed her hopes.

So after all he wasn't planning future breakfasts with her. Well, she would just have to make the most of this one. She piled her bluebell-patterned tray with most of her strawberry-patterned china, and carried it back. He accepted it with a word of thanks, and started opening his paper bags to set out crusty rolls, butter, paper-thin slices of rosy Ardennes ham...

'My usual breakfast is one roll, and jam, and coffee,' she told him severely.

He paused over the arrangement of a piece of Gruyère
cheese, shaking his head in disapproval. 'You might as
well fetch the jam, though. We might want it.'

It was strawberry, so at least it matched the dish she
spooned it into. She returned and set it next to the crois-
sants, her small contribution to the feast. Then she had
to pour the coffee, and organise the machine to make
two more cups, and then at last she could accept the
chair he pulled out for her.

'No Camembert?' she asked, surveying the plate where
a piece of Edam had been added to the Gruyère.

'I did think of it.' He pulled out another chair at her
side, and sat down. 'But you've had a bad record on
Camembert. Now, dormouse——'

'Would you mind not calling me that?' she asked dif-
fidently. 'I've, sort of, made some new resolutions.'

'Tell me about them,' he commanded, offering her
the basket of rolls. 'I always cut mine with a sharp knife,'
he observed as he helped himself in his turn, 'to keep
the crust whole...'

'Food again,' she exclaimed in mock exasperation. 'As
we're on resolutions, don't you think you could make
some about that?'

'About food? Whatever for?'

'On second thoughts, maybe not.' Taffy had just tasted
her roll. 'Where did you get these?'

'My usual place. You're the one who's making resolutions, not me,' he added with perfect logic. 'You were
going to tell me about them.'

'You said I had to. I don't remember deciding if I
would.' But it was a brief rebellion, gone as fast as her
melting mouthful of roll and butter and Gruyère. 'I
thought I might work hard, and try and get on in my
job.'

'Very worthy.'

'And the same with . . . with life in general. Having . . .' She finished her coffee, and found as she had hoped that it gave her the strength to express the thought without pain or reproach. 'Having had time to think about it.'

Which was the nearest she could get to mentioning how he had left her alone all of yesterday. Not for her soul would she ask what he'd been doing. Maybe he hadn't been doing anything, just enjoying a quiet evening alone in his beautiful house. Or maybe he hadn't been alone . . . no, she mustn't think about that.

'You know what, dormouse?' He pushed forward his cup for his second coffee. 'I've been doing some thinking, too.'

She filled the cup, loving to serve him. While she poured, he idly lifted one of her curls in that way he had, and the familiar warmth tingled through her from the almost-touch.

'Sorry, I forgot.' His fingers absently ruffled the clustering hair at the nape of her neck. 'I'm not supposed to call you dormouse any more, am I?'

'It's all right.' She set down the coffee-pot, and resisted the urge to snuggle into that warm, mastering hand. 'You said you'd been thinking?'

'Yes. About this flat, and whether it's different enough from when . . .' He checked himself.

'You do like it better now?' she asked anxiously.

'What a question!'

'That's what you said on Sunday, before you . . .' But no, she wouldn't let herself reproach him with going away and leaving her. 'It's not really an answer, is it?' she went on. 'I still don't know if you like this flat better with . . . with *me* in it.'

'Of course I do. But it's still not enough different.'

And that was as much as she could get from him. When she tried to ask what he meant, he only looked at that wretched, governing watch, and said he just had time to jog home and dress for his first appointment of the day.

'And seeing you mean to get on in your job,' he added with only the least edge of irony, 'maybe you'd better start by being punctual. I'll go with you as far as the bridge.' And he rose, and drew her to her feet, and kissed her very gently.

Her flesh still leapt to his touch, but there was something easier about it now. When he padded at her side in his black T-shirt and running-trousers, she was conscious of his panther strength, but, just for now, she found she could glory in it.

Their ways divided at the grandly named Pont Grande Duchesse Charlotte, known to locals as the Red Bridge. Here, Paul turned to face Taffy, and took both her hands in his.

'You're free this evening, I hope?' He made it sound as if she'd better be. 'There's a picture I'd like your opinion of.'

'You would?' She blinked into sunlight grown suddenly brilliant, a park green as emeralds, a pigeon strutting by with a little rainbow round its neck. 'You really would?'

'On this one, you might really be able to help.' He kissed each of her hands, and dropped them. 'I'll pick you up over there——' the fine head made a sideways movement to indicate the European Centre over the bridge '—at...what time do you finish? Right,' when she had told him, 'I'll be there.'

'But I'd like to go home and change...'

'No need for that.' His eyes, dark amber now in the open daylight, flicked over her. 'You look very nice as you are.'

He raised a muscular arm in farewell, and loped superbly away. She stayed to watch his disappearing figure, the strong feet pounding the path, the arms moving piston-style in the rhythm of his interrupted morning exercise. Not till he was out of sight did she turn with a sigh to cross the bridge, and even then she had to pause in the middle of it to see if she could catch another glimpse of him. She couldn't, but took consolation in the Alzette glimmering far below like a strip of fallen sky. Then she trailed on to her imprisoning tower workplace.

'Kissing hands at the Red Bridge, in full view of the whole town,' the all discovering Kendra exclaimed in the course of the morning. 'Believe me, my dear, no good will come of it.'

'For heaven's sake, I only met him two and a half days ago.' Taffy got up from her desk meaning to leave the room and end the conversation, but somehow only floated to the window. 'Why should anything come of it?' she demanded, eyes straying from the flapping national flags to the flying clouds. 'Who cares whether it does or not?'

And she really didn't. She cared about nothing but this evening. Happiness was the exact moment when she finished for the day, and Reception rang to say he was waiting for her. She hurried to the lift without so much as a glance in a mirror, and found him pacing the huge lobby, ready to seize her hand and draw her outdoors into the sweet, singing wind, and out of that into the leather comfort of his car.

The picture turned out to be in an exhibition of work by local artists. A water-colour of the Alzette in the mists

of an autumn morning, it showed the fallen-sky river
gleaming under the arched span of a bridge between patterns of crowded, shining roofs and the occasional tawny-
leafed tree.

'How can you bear not to buy it?' Taffy demanded,
unable to take her eyes off it. 'If you don't, somebody
else is sure to.'

'I don't know.' He stood before it, sizing it up. 'I have
to be absolutely sure it's right. She has so much
already...'

'Who?' Taffy struggled to hide her shock that he
should be so openly considering this as a gift for another
woman. 'Claudia?'

He shook his head, still taken up with the painting.
'This isn't Claudia's kind of thing at all—though now
that you mention it——' he turned back to Taffy, his
eyes bright iron, bright amber in the white north light
of the gallery '—it might be nice to give her a little something to cheer her up. A ring, maybe...'

A ring. He would give Claudia Vaughn a ring, some
other unknown woman a beautiful painting, while to
Taffy he brought nothing but bread and butter, cheese
and ham...

And his company, she reminded herself, her spirits
lightening. That's worth more than all the rest.

'This picture,' she said aloud. 'Where is it to hang?'

'In the living-room at home, of course,' he answered
absently, his attention once more on the painting.

Home? Had she heard him right? How could he mean
it for his own house and yet be giving it away? Did this
unknown woman then have the right to come and go in
that secret little house by the river? The questions
plagued Taffy like wasps, but she kept them within
though they stung her to the heart.

'Do you think it's a good idea to put this painting there?' she asked with difficult ease. 'The real river's so near...'

'The Moselle, you mean?' He turned to her, puzzled. 'The public terrace looks out on it, of course...'

'How did we get to the Moselle?' Taffy interrupted, lost.

'That's home, Federange-sur-Moselle...' He turned, and saw her bewilderment. 'It's my mother's birthday next week.'

'It is?' Relief flooded through her, and with it a rush of high spirits. 'Well, if I were you I'd grab that picture while it's going.'

'No, I'll think it over a day or two more.' He took her hand and tucked it under his arm, walking her to the exit. 'You thought I meant my house here in town?'

She nodded, trotting to keep up with him. 'You do have one, don't you? It wasn't all a dream I had the other day...'

'Some dream.' His voice was suddenly close, for her only. 'Shall we go back there, and dream it again?'

'You ought to buy that painting.'

But her body gave her real answer. Her hand clung to that hard, warm arm, her feet hurried her along rejoicing. He took the car for a little way, then led her through the magic doorway, up the paradise staircase to the river room where evening blurred the dancing light of the great island bed. And there she presently closed her eyes, and gave herself up to him, and took him within her for that other, inner journey which tonight revealed new delights at every turn until she didn't think she could bear it. But she could, and more, and more, because it was Paul and she knew he would bring her safe through to the drowsy peacefulness at the other end. And he did.

'So much to find out,' she murmured later, lying in his arms in quiet darkness edged with the faint yellow of street-lights. 'Why was that so different, Paul?'

'Always the questions.' He smoothed her hip. 'I think that's one of the things I like about you, dormouse. You're never afraid to ask questions.'

'You don't answer them though, do you?' She let go of him and turned on to her back, chilled by that little word 'like'. 'Why *was* it so different just now? I really want to know.'

'Perhaps it's because——'

He paused to kiss her temple and she waited, breathless. Would he find in himself what her own body already knew, that it was different now because now they belonged together?

'——because now we have time on our side,' he finished, his lips against her cheek.

It wasn't the answer she wanted, and yet she could see what he meant. Her prim skirt and blouse weren't all anyhow on the floor tonight, they were on a hanger in his dressing-room next to his suit. There'd been time for that, as now there was time to let passion rest, and think of other things. The trouble lay in having so much she didn't want to think of.

'I don't believe time's ever on our side,' she retorted, swallowing her disappointment. 'There's always something. For instance, you're sure to be hungry in a minute.'

'I'm hungry now.' He sat up, and put his feet on the floor. 'I got some supplies in specially.'

'Why, Paul Seyler,' she murmured, lazily watching the great dark figure operating the chaste strip-blinds to cover the window, 'you planned this.'

'I did.' He leant across her to the wall-light over the bed, and clicked it to bright, gentle life. 'We don't want to go out to supper tonight, do we?'

He didn't want to dress either, she discovered. He lent her a dark, thyme-scented silk robe, and himself pulled on another of those T-shirts, dark blue this time, and a fresh pair of tracksuit trousers. Thus attired, they ate from their laps on the high-backed settle in the living-room, fetching more from the kitchen as they needed it. Taffy sampled the smoked salmon, but refused the *foie gras* in favour of a salad of shrimps and avocado. Paul had some of everything, with liberal slices from a round dark loaf which he cut with a long shining knife. When she asked about wine he said he wasn't wasting any more on her until he had time to teach her how to drink it, and suddenly the Evian tasted like wine anyway.

'That was delicious.' She gathered up the napkin he had given her. 'Shall we sweep up the crumbs?'

'No need.' He took her plate with his own. 'Madame Thill can do that in the morning... My neighbour. We met her in the street on Sunday, remember?' And he called out something more as he disappeared into the kitchen.

'What was that you said?'

Taffy found she could hardly breathe. She stared up into the knowing eyes of the Cranach Venus, and just couldn't believe it. But then, look at this little black girl cuddling her lamb. Perhaps it was true after all, what he had just shouted so casually from the kitchen?

'Say it again,' she begged when he reappeared. 'I don't know that I heard it right.'

'What in particular?' he asked, puzzled.

'About Madame Thill coming in and tidying round for you every day.'

'Is that so odd?'

'No, no!' She shook her head impatiently. 'It was the other thing. Please, please, say it again!'

'About her being the only woman I've ever allowed in here besides you?'

'That was it,' Taffy breathed out in a great, rapturous sigh.

CHAPTER EIGHT

'IT'S snowing!' Taffy let go of a handlebar to capture a shining white flake on the Christmas-green and scarlet of her mitten. 'Now why couldn't it do this at the start of the weekend, instead of so late on Saturday?'

Paul had drawn ahead, as he was apt to do on his own streamlined bicycle. His feet in their dark trainers idled on the pedals, waiting for her to catch up, but she was in no hurry. From here she could enjoy his long, dark-trousered legs, his leather-gloved hands sure on the handlebars, his straight back flaring from narrow waist to broad shoulders in the crazy blue and white striped sweater which had the gold-crowned, red Luxembourg lion rampant on the front.

'If it had snowed earlier——' he turned his head, the blue striped knitted bonnet low and rakish over his forehead '—we couldn't have cycled.'

'We could have skied.' She glanced up at the beech trees arching overhead. 'These woods must be perfect for *langlauf*.'

'We'll get our long-distance skiing. Patience, dormouse.'

Patience. He was always saying that, yet surely he knew how patient she was being? She simply didn't know where she had found the patience to last this long with him on this basis. Here they were in January, and still he'd never...

No and no and no again, she scolded herself. I mustn't think like this.

Instead, she would concentrate on the good things. They'd canoed, and wind-surfed, and played tennis and squash with other couples in the clubs he belonged to. He'd even taken her horse-riding, though he hadn't enjoyed that as much as she had.

'It's not the same when the horse isn't your own,' he'd told her, and would say no more.

She could understand that, but still didn't know if he did have a horse, or horses, of his own. If so, he must keep them in the place he never took her, the place he wouldn't talk about. On some horrible weekends he would disappear from Friday evening to Monday morning, and then she would know that he had to be at Federange-sur-Moselle, she would just know it...

There I go again, she thought, and forced her mind back to the here and now.

The winter woods had their own stark beauty. This morning the air had been like chilled wine, and now, soft with snow, it was still a pleasure to breathe. On Friday they'd danced till the early hours, and sleepily breakfasted, and wandered up the paradise staircase to a morning bedtime so blissful that two hours' sleep had seemed more than enough.

And last week he'd taken her for the first time to his fencing-club. Her heart lifted with the memory of how, after several bouts of graceful, white-suited sparring, he'd taken off his mask and smiled across at her from under his black, plastered hair. She had run to him at once with his towel, and he'd drawn her to his heated body and kissed her, right there in front of everybody. Was that the action of someone who didn't want the world to know they were...?

That we're what? her tired brain nagged. What are we? He's never even said he...

But no, she dared not even think that word. He never spoke it and neither must she, or come anywhere near it.

She could express it in other ways though, and did. In early December she had spent all of one lonely weekend knitting that ski-bonnet as a worthy companion to his favourite heraldic sweater. When she gave him it as a Christmas present it seemed to please him, and in return he'd given her a package so small that her breath had caught in her throat as she unwrapped it.

But the little silk-lined box had held only a scarf-pin. She wore it all the time now, the gold, bushy-tailed dormouse with the green-jewel eyes he called spinel, but, but, but...

Spinel, she thought as the cycle-track started to rise. I don't rate precious stones, only semi-precious. And he'll take me anywhere, except the place that matters most to him.

This was only one of many expeditions they'd made to towns and villages of the Grand Duchy. She'd liked them all, Clervaux and Larochette, Beaufort and Diekirch, but they were never Federange-sur-Moselle. As if he wanted to keep her as far from there as possible, they'd never gone to the Moselle at all. When she'd suggested they take that direction this time, he had vetoed it at once.

'No, we'll go the other way. It's time you saw Vianden.'

So they'd driven to Echternach, then cycled the thirty-one kilometres upriver through the woods to Vianden's winding, cobbled streets. And, just as he forecast, she loved its pale-washed church with the tiled steeple, its castle with the tiled towers, its *stadhous* with the tiled dome, and, presently, the restaurant with the dining-room built over the river. The chef-proprietor of this place had chatted for an unusually long time, and had left Paul almost wistful.

'We were talking about this year's Elbling. That's a wine, you little savage,' as he saw her bewilderment. 'He bought some from us...that's to say,' he corrected himself with a sigh, 'from my mother.'

'You sound as if you wish it had been you.'

'Once a vintner, always a vintner,' her murmured, dark eyes fixed on some unshared inner vision. 'Ah, well. It can't be long now...' With a little shake of his head, he turned the pages of his menu faster than he needed to. 'What about the *pintade à la Luxembourgeoise*?'

Taffy left her own menu unopened. 'What can't be long now?'

'Or there's the *poularde au Riesling*...'

'If you want to settle down at...at *home*——' she forced out the painful word '—and run the vineyard, why don't you? What's stopping you?'

Was it because of her? Was he only waiting for this affair to burn out, for them to drift apart into their separate lives, before he did the thing he most wanted, and took over the reins at Federange? Dry-mouthed, she scanned him for clues. The full lips stayed pulled-in and straight, and while he studied the menu like that she couldn't see the iron and amber eyes.

'What,' she persisted, facing all the cruel answers he might give her, 'is stopping you?'

'Questions, questions.'

So as usual he gave her no answer at all. And somehow she wasn't as hungry as she thought. She made sure her omelette had only two eggs, but even then she could hardly finish it.

Why did he keep such an important part of his life shut off from her? It could only mean that, when the time came, he would return to Federange without her.

She was nothing but a brief city passion, the foreigner who for a while had caught his fancy before he returned to the land and the river where he'd always belonged. And if that left her with nowhere to go, nothing to do for the rest of her empty existence, well, that was the luck of the game she'd started so lightly five months ago.

I wish I'd never met him, she thought, cycling back along the River Our in the darkening afternoon. Don't I?

And because she couldn't lie to herself, she tried for some cheerful comment to make aloud.

'This is a land of rivers, isn't it?' She drew level with him, and waved sideways to where the pewter-glowing Our flowed towards its confluence with the Sûre under the snow-heavy sky. 'You'd think there'd be nothing lovelier than this, but Kendra says the Moselle's just glorious...'

She broke off, her front wheel wavering as she shot him a guilty sideways glance. And yet why should she feel guilty, just at mentioning Luxembourg's best-known river? He couldn't possibly know the rest of that conversation.

'Go and see it for yourself,' Kendra had urged as long ago as November. 'I'm not saying take the conducted tour of the *caves* like Annette did——'

'I should think not,' Taffy had interrupted, hitting three letters at once on her keyboard. 'Anyway, I couldn't now. Those tours finish at the end of October.'

'So you've thought of it?' shrewd Kendra retorted. 'There's nothing to stop you just visiting the district.'

'Yes, there is.' Taffy grimly typed the wrong word, grimly deleted it. 'I'm much too busy.'

'Busy having your time wasted,' Kendra had muttered.

Taffy knew exactly what she meant. To her older, happily married friend, time spent with a man who wouldn't marry you was time lost from a man who would.

Which in this day and age was an absurd way to think. Wasn't it?

Taffy shot another sideways glance at Paul, and saw with relief that he was smiling. Well, almost smiling, a lift at the corner of his mouth while his eyes stared ahead through the ever falling snow.

'Yes, the Moselle's glorious,' he began, feet steady on the slow pedals. 'Though I suppose I'm biased, seeing...' He turned his head for a brief glance, dark eyes warm in the surrounding chill. 'Seeing it's home. My father never left it for more than a day in his life.'

Taffy took a deep breath of the hushed, snow-filled air. He spoke so seldom of his family that when he did her mind eagerly hoarded every word. Thus she knew that he had only the one sister, who was Nick's mother, and no brothers. She knew that the vineyard had been in the family for five generations, and that his mother now managed it alone. Apart from the bare fact that his father had died two years ago, she couldn't remember Paul ever speaking of that relationship at all.

'Your father never left Federange?' she softly prompted. 'Not even for a holiday?'

'"Who needs holidays?" he used to say.' The strong feet slowed on the pedals, as though his energy were directed elsewhere. 'I don't think he ever came to terms with my making all this money.'

'You mean——' she let her own feet rest, not wanting the moment to end even though the snow was collecting on her Christmas-tree-green sweater '—he didn't like you getting rich?'

'He respected it.' Paul threw her another glance, an amber glint in the white, snowy light. 'But he was sad that it kept me from working along with him.'

'And your mother?' Taffy dared to ask.

'Drives a hard bargain.' Another, brighter glance, and an ironically affectionate smile as he set his front wheel to the whitened incline. 'Come on. I need to ring home.'

She toiled after him, chilled and weary. There he went again, not even knowing how he was shutting her out. She could come and go freely in the house by the Alzette, but home was Federange, and to Federange she was never invited.

Was it something about herself that was wrong? Yet he took her everywhere else, even last week to the Château de Betzdorf on that privileged advertiser's viewing of the Astra satellite station superbly housed in what had once been a grand-ducal residence. It was only Federange which was denied to her, only Federange which made him so cautious and evasive.

Only! Her angry feet drove at the pedals. If he wouldn't take her to his home, the place he really lived, what was the point of anything else?

It wasn't just Kendra who had sounded that Cassandra-note of warning. Taffy's brother Allen, driving her back to Kent for Christmas three weeks ago, had been equally disapproving.

Allen had started out from his own place in Strasbourg before dawn. That would have meant navigating Luxembourg at the height of the morning traffic, so Paul had volunteered to shorten his own daily jog to drive Taffy out for breakfast at a little inn near the motorway junction.

There Allen had presently joined them, and grudgingly accepted a quick coffee. Clipped and abrupt, he had spoken so little that she'd been almost glad when he pushed away the last of his coffee and told her it was time to be off. It was the start of a week's separation from Paul, and their farewells had had to be brief and restrained, but perhaps that was just as well.

'I hope you know what you're doing, Taff,' Allen had begun as soon as they were on the motorway.

Alarmed, Taffy had realised at last what was troubling her over-protective brother. He was assuming that she and Paul had spent the night together. And how could she contradict, when it was the simple truth?

'I'm a big girl now,' she pointed out instead. 'I can take care of myself.'

'Huh. That guy's a bit smart for my taste.'

'Only you——' Taffy nodded towards her brother's five-year-old sweater, and the battered anorak on the back seat '—could talk about somebody in a tracksuit being too smart.'

'There's tracksuits and tracksuits,' Allen muttered darkly. 'And that car——'

'Saved you some weary city driving,' Taffy cut in crisply. 'You could try being a bit grateful.'

Allen had stayed silent for a while, but he wasn't done with her. 'Now I see,' he announced presently, 'why I always get that blasted answering-machine when I try to ring you.'

'I always call you back,' Taffy defended herself.

'You're sure he isn't married or anything?'

'Quite sure. I've met lots of his friends...'

'Woman friends, or just the men?'

'He's not keeping me like a *demi-mondaine*, you know,' Taffy burst out in exasperation. 'It's all perfectly respectable.'

'Have you met his family?'

'Y-yes.' After all, she'd met Paul's cousin Nick.

'How did they treat you?' her bulldog brother persisted.

'They're fine,' she parried. 'Not forever interfering and asking questions, like mine.'

But Allen wouldn't be deflected. 'Did you pay them a Christmas visit? Did you, Taff?'

'You know what Christmas is like,' she floundered. 'Strictly family...'

'You didn't,' he concluded, eyes on the road. 'Have you written or said anything to the folks about this guy?'

'N-no.'

Her parents called once a week, always at the same time. It had been quite easy to organise being at home for that, and equally easy to avoid mentioning Paul to them in her letters.

'Then I won't either,' Allen decided, closing ranks as usual with his own generation. 'But you've still got three brothers, Taff. I'll let Chris and Richie know what's going on.'

'*Nothing's* going on!' she snapped.

To no avail. On the return journey, Allen had insisted on bringing her right back to her flat, and, once there, had sniffed into every corner of every room.

He wouldn't find any trace of Paul that way, Taffy reflected now amid the hypnotically whirling snow. She hardly ever slept there herself, let alone with company.

'Tired?' Paul's voice sounded deeper than ever through the snowy hush. 'You should have eaten more.'

'We can't all burn off the extra calories the way you do.' She licked a snowflake off her lip. 'I suppose there's no chance of our eating at my place tonight?'

'Another two-egg omelette?' he teased.

'Smoked trout,' she told him with dignity. 'I bought enough for two, but I dare say I needn't have bothered. I don't believe you trust my cooking.'

'You smoked these trout yourself?'

'I'd make a horseradish-and-apple sauce to go with it. You're dodging again.'

He turned to stare at her in surprise. 'I'm what?'

'Dodging real things by being jokey.'

'*Touché*, dormouse.' He sounded a little shaken.

Taffy herself was shaken. She'd never dared reproach him like this before. Until she'd heard herself putting her complaint with such crude precision, she hadn't even known she was thinking it.

Why was her mind suddenly so clear? Was is something about their smooth progress through this ever falling, ever renewed snow? They had left the village of Reisdorf now and were back in sombre woods where the branches had narrowed to a black and silver web, and the usual woodland noises had all stilled. She could hear nothing but the tiny crackle of snow compacting under their wheels. They might have been sailing through the white clouds of limbo to the land of heart's desire.

Heart's desire? Some chance, thought Taffy. And yet, maybe now I can say things I couldn't say before.

'So is it my cooking?' she asked aloud. 'Because, if so, you shouldn't knock it till you've tried it.'

Perhaps the silence and the snow had affected Paul, too. Perhaps that was why he had suddenly spoken of his father a few kilometres back, after all these months of never mentioning him. Perhaps that was why he was ready to answer her with such sober honesty, feet steady on the pedals for the easy downhill run.

'It's not your cooking.'

At any other time, Taffy knew she would have demanded to know what was it, then? Here and now though she could coast at his side, and let the snow fall, and let him take his time.

'I...I never feel comfortable in that building these days,' he said at last.

Questions crowded upon her, but she held them back. They could wait. The river had darkened from pewter to black, and what light there was came from the whiteness below, a world turned upside-down.

'Whenever I'm there, it reminds me of...'

He stopped for so long, she wondered if he had changed his mind about whatever he wanted to say. She kept her hands loose in the mittens, and controlled the tension she could feel at the back of her shoulders. He'd just spoken of his father for the first time ever. Had he now, after five months' silence, almost brought himself to speak of Claudia?

Her only news of the singer had come in the most impersonal manner possible.

'So it really was an ulcer,' she'd called through the open doorway of Paul's dressing-room on their second Sunday morning together. 'It says so here.'

'In the paper?' he'd answered from among his jackets. 'Then it must be true, mustn't it?'

'She's cancelled her European tour——'

'Shall I wear an English tweed this morning, dormouse?'

'—and gone to recover at her home in Arizona.' Taffy had lowered the paper. 'I hope she gets well there.'

'What's our weather report for today?'

'Don't you care about your friend who's ill?'

At that, he'd straightened from the clothes-rack and turned to face her, tall and forbidding in his ochre roll-necked shirt and coffee-coloured trousers. It had been one of the moments, Taffy recalled, when she'd been almost afraid of him.

'Surely——' she'd begun in what she could recognise now as a nervous, self-justifying babble '—surely I'm entitled to be glad she's well enough to leave hospital?'

'You are, dormouse.' And he'd turned away to take the tweed jacket from its hanger. 'I thought we might breakfast in the Place d'Armes this morning...'

He's always done that, Taffy thought as the snow squeaked under her wheels. He's always changed the subject when it was something he didn't want to talk about.

This time, he seemed to have simply decided to say no more. And after all, he'd talked of his parents, and indirectly of his life at Federange.

That's already progress, she told herself, floating through snowy limbo. I mustn't be greedy.

And at last it came, like a reward for patience. 'That flat of yours always reminds me of Annette.'

Taffy was unaware of her sigh of relief until she felt it loosening all her muscles, and settled her suddenly easy shoulders. 'Why didn't you tell me? I could have moved.'

The blue-striped cap turned, the eyes below it pools of shadow. 'You don't mind my being reminded of Annette?'

She shook her own head, placid and secure. 'You don't sound as if you like being reminded of her.'

'I don't, but I couldn't ask you to move just for that. And besides——' his eyes returned to the snowy track '—it hardly seemed worthwhile.'

'Why not?' She clutched the handlebars tight, yet this new, snow-gifted courage kept her voice steady. 'Because you don't expect us to be going on much longer?'

'What on earth gives you that idea?'

His tone was so surprised, the question so welcome, that her balance failed. Some small, snow-covered unevenness in the track threw her to one side, and before she knew it she had wavered and fallen to the white-cushioned verge. Perhaps it was more than snow, or moss under the snow, that cushioned her fall, she reflected as she lay there perfectly comfortable and unhurt. Perhaps it was sheer happiness.

'Are you all right?' Strong hands raised the bicycle off her, then took her by the waist and pulled her gently to her feet. 'You didn't hit this tree?'

He pushed her against its rough bark and stayed there, walling her in. She blinked down at the crowned lion on his chest, black now against dark and white stripes.

'I'm fine, honest. Better than fine,' she added softly as she remembered the words that had so astonished her. 'Would you mind just saying that again?'

'Saying what again?' he demanded impatiently. 'Are you sure you're all right? You fell right by this damn tree...'

'It's a heavenly tree.' She threw away her mittens, threw her arms round his neck. 'Everything is. Here and now, everything's just perfect.'

And she drew his darkness down to where she could lose herself in it. His cheeks were cool and rough and scented with wild thyme, his lips and tongue hot, his head warm to her fingers where she slid them under the dark and light striped cap. His hands caressed her, strong and gentle through all the layers of clothing, his gloves and her trousers and sweater...

No, wait, he wasn't wearing his gloves. He must have got rid of them as she had, and now his warm hands had somehow found their way under her sweater, and under her T-shirt. They moved up over her bare, joyful skin, and freed her hot breasts for his pleasure and hers.

Her breathing grew tremulous and ragged. She felt his lips hot on her cheek and neck, his hands hot on her covered breasts, and now on her uncovered thighs which had no choice but to open and welcome this other heat of his to where it belonged, deep within her, deep and hot and perfect in the snow-covered, perfect world. She flowed to him and round him and with him, ever stronger, ever faster, until their flow ended in flying whiteness which gradually settled to silver, and they drifted back to earth to find the snow had stopped, and the moon come out.

'Out in the forest, for goodness' sake,' Taffy murmured as she tugged her clothes into some kind of order. 'What if anybody had seen us?'

'We could have been treating each other for frostbite.' The deep voice suggested a smile in the strange, white-barred darkness. 'We did have all our clothes on.'

'Or nearly all.' She dreamily accepted the mittens he had picked up for her. 'Enough to be...'

'Hell!'

'What is it?' Taffy came to startled attention.

She had been watching his hands putting on his gloves. Whitened by a filtered chink of moonlight, they had patted the leather snug over his fingers, settled his thumb in its special-shaped covering...

'Oh!' She felt her eyes widen, trying to read the black, moon-flecked outline of his face. 'You didn't...'

'Exactly. I didn't.'

Was it anger in the deep voice? Regret? Both, Taffy decided, and more which she couldn't interpret, struggling as she was with her own tangled emotions.

She bowed her head, guilt-stricken. 'I should have started taking the Pill.'

'Could have, should have, might have... Come on.' He picked up her bicycle, and dusted snow off the seat. 'Let's get this back where it belongs, and take it from there.'

How like him, she thought as she remounted and coasted with him beside the hurrying Sûre. No inquests, no blame, no what-ifs—just on with whatever happens to need doing here and now.

Which is all very well, her confused mind argued back, but I'm still left with a great big what-if of my own.

No, he's right, she decided as the lights of Echternach glowed in the distance. It might never happen.

But if it did, would he stand by her? Would her marry her?

But I don't want him like that, she realised in anguish, not a shotgun wedding! That way, I'd never find out if he really...

And here it was again, the word he had never spoken, the word she daren't even think in case it tempted fate. The longing for it came at her through all the casual, friendly chat at the place where they returned her hired bicycle, and again as she waited for him to fix his own bicycle in its special car-rack, and again in the car as he keyed a number into the phone, and waited, and keyed again, and still got no reply.

'I'll try later.' He replaced the phone it its cradle between them.

'Back there in the forest,' Taffy heard herself with horror, but couldn't stop, 'when I fell, and you picked me up, and... and what happened next. What would you call that?'

'I don't know.' He turned on the deep leather seat, yellow-lit by a street-lamp which shone through the windscreen. 'It's not like anything I've ever done before, dormouse.'

'I'd call it...'

But she couldn't after all say it. I'd call it love, she'd wanted to say, but it wouldn't come out. It stuck in her throat, her breath rushing past it unused. She turned imploring eyes on him in the darkness, but he wasn't even thinking of what she was trying to say. He was thinking—she heard him with outraged disbelief—he was thinking about *food* again!

'That smoked trout.' He was clearly turning the idea over in his mind. 'How long would it take you to make the sauce?'

'No time at all,' she snapped. 'I've got the ingredients, and a food-processor that badly needs exercise.'

'You like cooking?' he asked, very softly.

'What do you care? You've got all your restaurants that feed you like a king...'

'Maybe it's time for changes, dormouse.'

Taffy blinked. 'What changes?'

'I've been selfish.' Again that softness in the deep voice, the low, intimate note he usually kept for bed. 'Never meeting you on your own ground, never accepting your way of doing things... I'll have to watch that.'

'Never letting me cook for us in my own kitchen, you mean?'

Taffy found that her own voice had softened. She had the strangest feeling that their minds were more in harmony than she had understood, that his talk of food was simply his own way of approaching a subject as difficult and important to him as it was to herself.

'And not only that. I've noticed,' he went on, 'how often you've needed, oh——' he sought for examples '—shoes, your hair-drier, a letter—and they were back in your own flat.'

'It does happen.' She was conscious of weighing each word carefully. 'But it's worth it, to——' To be with you: the words ached unspoken in her throat '—to spend time in that beautiful house,' she finished instead.

'Beautiful it may be, but it's no place to...'

Now it was his turn to break off. Could he, too, be rejecting whatever he'd meant to say, and be looking for something to put in its place? In the silence she heard the tiny, crackling patter of new snow feathering the windscreen, closing up their view, shutting them off from the outside world.

'We'd better get going.' And he was suddenly, energetically busy, finding his keys, switching the dashboard to green and red life, clicking on his safety-belt.

Seething with frustration, she put on her own belt. He had started the heater with the fan full on the windscreen, and set the wipers going. Already the magic snowflakes had blurred; soon they would be a mere dribble, and there he went with that wretched phone again. Something new had just been about to happen between them, she was sure of it, though she didn't know what because of this pretend urgency—yet still he had to talk to Federange. For heaven's sake, what did he need to hear from there that was so important?

Whatever it was, he didn't hear it—the number still didn't reply. He replaced the phone, and manoeuvred them out of the village and on to the main road back to the city. The snow under their wheels was already blackened by traffic, reduced to a mere nuisance, and yet she had to try once more for the mood it had created, back there in the forest.

'You were saying something about your house,' she began, trying to control her breathing.

'Was I?' He didn't take his eyes from where the headlights had turned the snow into a pale yellow, confusion-weaving enemy. 'Oh, yes. I was saying that it was no place to—er—to cook.' His hand left the gear-lever for a moment, and sought hers. 'I fancy that smoked trout, dormouse.'

She let her breath out easier, let herself relax. She knew this wasn't what he'd meant to say, but it was something, his own style of approach which she must respond to. She mentally reviewed the contents of her store-cupboard.

'I'll make onion soup for starters.'

He shot her a quick glance, the tip of his tongue between his lips. 'With toasted rounds of bread and cheese?'

'Honestly, Paul after all that lunch!' she laughed, spirits soaring. 'It just isn't fair, the way you never put on weight.'

The satisfaction of it lasted the rest of the journey. For the first time ever, it was *her* cooking he was looking forward to with such pleasure. The meal she had promised him tonight was simple enough, but that was only the beginning. On Monday, she would buy all she needed for her real speciality, the steak and kidney pudding with oysters her mother had taught her, and serve it with the very best vegetables the market could provide...

'Goodness, are we there already?' She blinked up at the familiar apartment-block. 'Will you garage the car?'

'You mean, am I staying the night? That depends.'

And he took up the phone yet again, and yet again tried to get through to Federange. Taffy listened to the little penetrating unanswered buzz at the other end, and wondered yet again about this vital news that he needed so much to hear.

He recradled the phone at last. 'I'd better try the——'

He bit the sentence off so sharply that Taffy almost fancied she could hear his teeth closing on it. His head was turned towards her in the shadows, and though she couldn't see his features, she could feel the tension in him.

'Why don't we go up anyway?' she began timidly. 'You can use my phone——'

She got no further. He had leapt from the car and slammed the door, cutting off her words. Whatever that news was, she decided miserably as she watched him hurrying round to the pavement, he really needed it.

Then she saw the reason for his haste. Two women had appeared in the lit doorway of the apartment block, wrapped against the cold yet each conveying somehow, perhaps in the way they stood, perhaps by the mere angle of their heads, that same tension she had sensed in Paul. He had already reached them, and the majestic, white-haired older one was addressing him in rapid Letzeburgesch. The other was...

Taffy stared, and got out of the car, and stared again. That headscarf let out only the tiniest hint of ash-blonde hair, and enormous, dark-rimmed spectacles almost eclipsed the tilted eyes, but there was no mistaking Claudia Vaughn.

'What is it? What's going on?'

Taffy crossed to the group, but nobody took any notice of her. Left behind like a forgotten piece of luggage, she looked on in misery while Paul put an arm round Claudia's luxuriously full mink coat, picked up the little suitcase at her side, and tenderly supported her to his car. The other woman went with them, watchful on Claudia's other side, and when Paul had Claudia settled in the front seat, he opened the back door of the car for this other passenger.

Only then did he pause to glance in Taffy's direction. 'You'd better go on up. I'll get back to you when I can——'

'You will not,' the old woman interrupted harshly, in English, through the still open door of her back seat. 'You will stay where it is right for you to be, with the woman who is bearing your child.'

CHAPTER NINE

FOR a moment Taffy couldn't take it in. She shut her eyes tight and shook her head to clear it, but when she looked again, nothing had changed. The car was still at the kerb, Paul's streamlined bicycle still fastened to it to prove that long ago, in another life, he and she had floated together through the timeless, snowy forest, closer than ever before...

She shuddered from the pain of it. Minutes ago, in that car, he had talked of their future together. Now, he had given her place in it to a woman with a far better right, the best right in the world, to be at his side for the rest of his life.

She stared across the pavement at the sleek lines of the car. While Claudia waited shadowy and silent in the front seat, Paul rasped something ferocious in his own language through the rear door to the old woman within, who answered in the same tone.

That's his mother, Taffy realised. I suppose he's angry with her for giving the game away to me.

So his mother was somehow involved in looking after the mother of his child. Had Claudia then been at Federange all this time? Was that why he'd always refused to say a word about her? Was that why he'd always gone there alone?

No wonder he didn't want *me* there, Taffy realised, pain lancing through her like a white laser beam. No wonder he never talked about the place, or any plans he might have to live there.

Even today, in that new closeness which had become such an agonising, white-lit memory, even then he had dodged the subject, accomplished two-timer that he was. Yes, she could see it now. This harsh white insight might hurt, but at least it helped her to understand the cold, cruel, selfish schemer who was the real Paul Seyler.

Look at him now, cutting short his mother's angry words by banging the car door. And now he was tapping on Claudia's window, and when it was lowered, murmuring something private...

I can't watch this, Taffy thought. I've got to get away.

But she couldn't. When Paul crossed the slushy pavement to her with that panther stride, when he stood over her like this, he filled her world as full as ever. His treacherous eyes were dark hollows in the street-light, but still the lithe body moved with athletic grace in that lion-crested sweater she had laughed at so tenderly, still the black hair swirled over his forehead and ears in that heartbreaking, uncharacteristic wildness...

'Where is it?' Her own voice echoed dull and accusing through the chaos inside her head. 'Where's your cap?'

'What?' A frown gathered over the hard-etched nose, a new darkness between the dark of hair and eyes. 'What on earth——?'

'Ah, yes, you took it off in the car. You threw it on the back seat.' She swallowed, determined to make herself accept the truths newly revealed by this harsh inner light. 'I suppose that's where I've always belonged with you. In a back seat...'

'We've no time for this.' The deep voice thrust hers aside. 'Claudia's just started labour. My mother was going to call the ambulance when she saw me arriving.'

'Why here?' Taffy heard her tone change from dully accusing to dully questioning. 'Why isn't she having the baby where it belongs, at Federange——?'

She broke off, as his mother lowered her window to call some sharp comment. He snapped a reply, and turned again to Taffy.

'Forget Federange. She's booked into the place that saved the baby five months ago.'

'So that's what it was. Threatened miscarriage.' Taffy swallowed down the bitterness. 'And you knew it.'

'I knew it because she'd just told me, that night. Women!' He hadn't even the grace to be guilty, merely exasperated. 'She ignores her pregnancy for four months, and then suddenly the baby's the earth and sky...'

'That was quite a night for us both, wasn't it?' She spoke to fight off the pain. 'I lost my virginity, you found you were to become a father——'

'What?' His astonished impatience cut her short. 'Surely I don't have to tell you, of all people, that it isn't my child?'

'No?' She pretended to consider. 'But then, that's just what you would say. To me, that is,' she added with her bleak new vision. 'Before you go to be with her at the birth——'

'I'll do no such thing,' he barked in rising fury. 'The hospital waiting-room is as far as I go.'

'Not that it's any of my business,' Taffy went on in that hating, hateful, questioning tone, 'but seeing she's here, why did you keep phoning Federange?'

'That's where she was until this afternoon, when she insisted on coming here ready,' he explained, for all the world as if he were on the outside of this pregnancy instead of in the middle of it. 'As it turns out, she was right.'

This afternoon. So while Paul and Taffy had been making hot, hot love in the cold, cold forest, Claudia had been packing her bag for the maternity ward.

'Why weren't you with her?' Taffy choked, driven at last to the central knot of her misery. 'It's all bad, awful, but you being with me when she's so near her time, that's the worst.'

'I tell you again, Taffy——' he paused to throw an urgent glance back at the car '—*this is not my child*!'

'So your mother wasn't speaking the truth?' Taffy wouldn't meet those smudges of darkness which were his lying eyes. 'It must run in the family.'

'Stop this! Stop it at once!' His rage thundered through the snowy street, bringing startled glances from both of the women in the car. 'I am not a liar, and neither is my mother,' he added in a suppressed undertone. 'She's simply knowing best, like her usual stubborn self.'

'And why is she so sure?'

'That's easy.' The blue and white stripes rippled, the red lion's gold crown and gold claws glittered with his impatient shrug. 'When a man brings home a beautiful, pregnant woman——'

'Beautiful,' Taffy repeated dully. 'Pregnant. To your home, where you never took me.'

'How could I, with my mother doing her damnedest to get me married to Claudia before the birth?'

Married. Taffy clutched her arms round her body, tight against the hurt. She had tried so hard not to think that word, not to hope it for herself, and now here he was, starkly and coldly throwing it at her about another woman.

'And are you?' She stopped, then forced herself to go on in a reluctant croak. 'Are you m-married?'

'Give me strength!' But he had plenty of that, banked down and ready to blow her over the roof-tops if he let go of it. 'Do you really think any woman, even my mother, could make me——?'

'And that's why you haven't m-m...' Here it came again, the laser-piercing word which must be faced, and conquered. 'Why you haven't m-married Claudia yet? To show them who's boss?'

'Idiot! As if I ever——'

'Or don't you believe her that the baby's yours?' The terrible word spoken, Taffy found it quite easy to keep going. 'Is she a liar too? It takes one to know one, they say——'

'Taffy, I swear if you call me that once more...' His hands rose to her shoulders to grasp and shake, but he stopped them in time. 'You're as bad as my mother,' he went on in that angry, controlled undertone. 'Jumping to conclusions, judging what you don't understand...I have never lied to you.' More banked-down power escaped in a ferocious hiss. 'Not even by——'

'Not even by telling me you were free when you so very much aren't?' She recalled her absurd last-minute question before the first time they'd ever...but no, she couldn't bear to think about it. 'That was a direct lie,' she tore on through the pain. 'But lots of times you've simply twisted the truth. Like when you convinced me Claudia was nothing to you.'

'I've never pretended that.' But he was more sober now, and defensive. 'How could I, when we've been...?'

He paused as if to spare her feelings, but she wouldn't have wanted them spared. With self-lacerating triumph, she finished the thought for him.

'When you've been lovers?'

'*No!*'

'Paul,' Claudia called thinly from her open car-window. 'I'm sorry, but we'd better go.'

'It's all right,' Taffy called gently back. 'I won't keep him any longer.'

The comforting note in her own voice astonished her. But Claudia had sounded so small, so worried, so much in awe of the overwhelming experience before her, that somehow gentleness and comfort were the only possible way to respond.

'Coming, *ma belle*,' Paul's deep voice chimed in, and he turned once more to Taffy. 'You hear how she is? If ever a woman needed taking care of——'

'Oh, come on!' Hearing that husbandly tone, the fond *'ma belle'*, Taffy felt suddenly, infinitely tired. 'You'd better get back where you belong. For what you're worth——'

'That's enough!' His hand whipped up to cover her mouth. 'You don't know what you're saying.'

'You're wrong there.' She twisted her head away from that cupped, thyme-scented hand so full of memories. 'This time, I know exactly what I'm saying, and exactly what I'm doing.'

'Listen, Taffy,' he began urgently, 'I give you my word——'

'I wouldn't.' She turned to face the length of the snowy, desolate street. 'I don't think your word's worth much.'

'Go in, and I'll get back to you,' he ordered as if he still had the right. 'We can't talk any more now, but——'

'But nothing!' She huddled away from him. 'If your own mother doesn't believe you, why should I?'

'Because I'm speaking the truth, you little——'

'Please, Paul!' Claudia called again. 'Please!'

The rising note of urgency stopped him in mid-sentence. Without another word he swung away, across the pavement, round the car, and into the driver's seat. The engine purred to life, the tyres hissed through the wet snow, and Paul Seyler, his mother, his mistress, and his approaching child glided to the corner out of sight.

And that's that, Taffy thought. It's over.

One day, she knew, she'd come to terms with it. Until then, well, she certainly wasn't going to do as Paul had told her, and return to her flat. She wasn't sure she'd ever go there again, to be reminded in a hundred subtle and not so subtle ways that yet another of his women had once lived there.

Maybe he's seeing Annette Warren too, she brooded. How would I know? I don't know anything about him.

So what *was* she going to do? See if Kendra was at home? The idea sent Taffy hurrying down the street in the opposite direction, escaping from the endless ways Kendra could say 'I told you so' and 'forget him' and 'he's not good enough for you'.

I know all that, she told herself, kicking up the slushy snow with her trainers. I just don't want to hear it aloud for a bit. Not for a bit ... And she thrust her hands in the pockets of her trousers, and wandered on through streets which, however busy on this early Saturday evening, still seemed drearily empty.

No wonder he was so careful about lovemaking, she thought savagely as she found herself at the beginning of the Red Bridge. He couldn't risk another mistake, could he? That was himself he was protecting, not me.

All but once. Her heart wrenched at the memory of that ecstasy in the snowy forest, but she grimly faced its possible consequences. If it did turn out that he'd fathered a child on her also, then she wouldn't even tell him. She'd go home ...

In fact I'll go home anyway, she decided, wandering on down any path her feet came to. What's to keep me here? I hate him, everything about him, everywhere I've been with him ...

Presently, it started snowing again. Fat feathers of it clung to the wool of her sweater, and melted, and soaked through the knitted fabric. Some distant part of her noted that it had begun trickling down her neck, and between her breasts, and that her feet were soaked as they slid about on the snowy cobbles of these narrow, winding ways between tall, old, narrow houses...

'So this was where I was heading,' Taffy said aloud.

She looked down at the wet hand she had taken from her wet pocket. Yes, it held her key, the key she had been so proud to accept from him in trust five months ago.

I should drop it in the Alzette, she thought, and then, as she let herself in, Why, I still could. Right out of his window.

She switched on the fountains of light among the wrought-iron foliage of the hall. The doe and her fawn still grazed by the door, the squirrel still harvested his apple. The lovingly feathered wooden doves still courted on their apple-bough over the concealed hook where her winter coat hung with his, trustingly next to the serpent in this paradise...

I could destroy all this, she thought, as he's destroyed me.

All of these animals were detachable. If she dropped them in the river they'd float for miles—he'd probably never get them back. His Trémont panther from the living-room would sink without trace, his paintings be completely ruined...

'As if I ever could,' she sighed aloud, and drifted to the living-room to address the loving little black girl and her lamb. 'Don't worry, my darlings, I'd never hurt you. Not even you,' she added to the cozening Cranach Venus. 'Though I can see now that you're the very woman for him, already without your clothes...'

Clothes! That was it, of course!

She pelted up the paradise staircase to his dressing-room, and flung back the gliding doors of his cupboards. Here they all were at her mercy, his beautiful suits, his heavy silk shirts, his designer pullovers... For a moment of unholy glee she relished the thought of everything waterlogged, ruined, even if he could rescue them before they sank.

Then the scent of wild thyme hit her. And here was her own flared dress she'd hung there last night, still with the arms of his favourite jacket over it where he'd playfully draped them, to take care of it, he'd said...

Tears burst forth at last. Giving herself up to noisy sobs, she grabbed a handful of his smooth-laundered, thyme-scented handkerchiefs, and staggered to the bedroom.

She was so cold, so tired, so wet. And though she knew she had no right to be here, that he'd never had the right to invite her here, yet this island bed was where she belonged.

'I hate him,' she said aloud as she kicked off her soaked trainers, peeled off her clinging-wet socks, and stamped out of her trousers and briefs without bothering to disentangle them.

Her wet sweater and T-shirt came off all in one, and dropped in a heap on the polished boards. Even her bra was wet, a relief to take off so that she could crawl, shivering and naked, under the wild-thyme-scented duvet.

'I do hate him, I do!' she insisted into the bundle of his handkerchiefs which had somehow stayed in her hand all through her undressing. 'If only I didn't lo-o-ove him so much...'

By the time she shook open the fifth and last handkerchief, her eyes were so hot that she had to close them.

She bunched the wet pillow under her cheek, dragged the duvet over her aching shoulders, curled her aching limbs round her aching heart, and let warmth and darkness take her in their care.

But her dreams knew what she really wanted, and gave it to her. So it seemed while she slept that he was here with her in the dark, as he so often had been.

It had nothing to do with passion, this way of being together. It could flame into passion at any time, but the best of it was just knowing he was here. His arm rested across her, his hand gently cupped one of her breasts, his naked legs tangled hard and warm with hers, his naked body followed the line of hers like a shield against the world.

She slept so easy when he was with her like this. And she didn't have to admit it was a dream, not yet, not till the river light winked and wavered round the edges of those closed strip-blinds, and it was morning...

And it was true. He was here. She could feel his warmth at her back, his arm across her body, his steady, sleeping breath fluttering her hair.

So it must have been the other that was a dream. The snowy street, the woman about to bear his child—what a nightmare! She sighed, and snuggled against him, and let herself drift up out of sleep as she so often had, here with him in this bed.

Her eyes were waking up now—why did they feel so heavy? And for some reason the light was extra bright this morning. She could easily see the little heaps of her yesterday's clothes, her trainers lying on their sides, the four handkerchiefs, the fifth a wet bundle here by her hand...

'You louse!' She shook off his arm, and whipped upright against the padded bedhead.

He didn't open his eyes, or come anywhere near waking. All he did was grunt a little, and fling the arm she had rejected back across her hips, to snuggle his face against her side. She had quite a fight to get away from him, but she managed, and swung her feet to the floor.

'Scum! Fink! Ratbag!' She spat the words out in a series of satisfying little explosions as her toes hit the polished boards. 'How you've got the nerve to——'

'Behave yourself, dormouse.'

The deep voice came out sleep-blurred, then muffled as he pulled the duvet over his head. She stared at the featureless mound with something between rage and tears. He couldn't cover all his great length at once, so now his feet stuck out, his strong, high-arched, flexible, liar's feet...

Her hand shot out to pull the duvet away, but she caught it back in time. She would wake him all right, and tell him the whole truth about himself, start to finish—but not yet. Not till she was dressed, or heaven knew what he'd be able to do to her. Already her body was preparing itself... She hurried into her still soaked T-shirt and scarcely less wet trousers, welcoming their clamminess against her rebellious body.

When she drew back the strip-blinds, she saw why the light was so brilliant. Snow sparkled on the window-sill, and the low sun turned the river to silver under the pale blue winter sky.

We'd have skated, she found herself thinking, or tobogganed. Or maybe just tramped about, and seen all the turrets and towers dreamier than ever in the snow...

She steeled herself against another of those endless waves of pain, and opened the window with new resolution. Not giving herself time to think, she grabbed up a double handful of snow, and dumped it full on the soles of Paul's exposed feet.

His first reaction was entirely satisfactory. His feet clenched, kicked off the snow, and vanished under the suddenly heaving duvet as his rumpled head emerged at its other end. When he shot upright, it began to seem not such a good idea after all. His bright-dark eyes snapped open and focused first on her, then on the open window, and then, in growing incredulous rage, on the little pile of snow soaking into the sheet.

He flung back the duvet cover with a roar. 'Why you...you...' He leapt at her, magnificently naked. 'I'll murder you!'

She turned to flee but that only made it easier for him to grab her wrists in one pitiless hand. His other clamped on the nape of her neck and forced her, struggling uselessly, to the still open window. Then he pushed her down to the snowy sill and somehow held her there while he dumped handfuls of snow in her hair and on the back of her neck.

'Stop it,' she gasped in a muffled gurgle. 'I hate you!'

He let her go. 'Is that you saying you're sorry?'

'It isn't, and I'm not.' She kept her head out, shaking snow from her tangled curls. 'I just woke you to tell you——'

'Woke me?' He dragged her in, and reached a muscular arm over her to bang shut the window. 'You damn near gave me a heart attack.'

'Don't make me laugh.' She dodged back from him, not laughing. 'You haven't got a heart,' she hurried on, determined not to be overawed by the sheer, naked, animal power of him. 'To come here and sleep beside me, like anybody decent!'

'Where the hell am I meant to sleep, if not in my own bed?' He ran a hand through his hair, leaving it more on end than ever. 'I didn't *get* here till four, thanks to you damned women——'

'The baby's born, then?' she asked, torn between her jealous envy of Claudia and her deep, feminine wonder at the age-old miracle of birth. 'They're all right?'

'They're fine.' He yawned and stretched hugely, almost to the glimmering ceiling. 'It's a girl. With, thank heaven, the reddest hair you ever saw.' And he actually smiled, if ruefully. 'There has never, thank heaven, been a red-haired Seyler.'

'There is now.'

'Don't give me all that again.' He dropped his arms, and took a step towards her. 'When I found you here, I thought it meant you'd come to your senses.'

'I've certainly done that...leave me alone!'

She backed away, clung to the wall, stayed as stiff and heavy as she could, but none of it worked. Those dear, strong arms scooped her as they always had to this dear, warm chest...

Where she'd no right to be. Where he'd no right to hold her, his every touch an outrage to all truth.

'Put me down!' She hammered at him with her fist.

Or rather, she meant to, if she could have made her hand accept the task. But it wouldn't. Instead, it opened wide for her fingers to explore the hard ridge of his collar-bone, the soft hair of his chest, the strong ribcage where his heart beat as clear and steady as if it belonged to an honest man.

'What on earth do you think you're doing, putting these wet things back on?' he demanded, his lips against her forehead. 'I suppose you walked here last night?'

She nodded, wet hair brushing his face. 'I didn't mean to.'

'No. Can you imagine what it's like, waiting for another man's child when your own woman's gone crazy?'

His own woman? She mustn't believe him. She mustn't ever let him take her in again, for all her own wretched heart flipped and flopped and fluttered down there under her breast. She put her hand over it, glad to chill it with the damp cotton of her T-shirt, and drew a long, ragged breath.

'If by your own woman you mean me, I haven't gone crazy. I've gone sane.'

'Sure, sure,' he soothed. 'It was very sane of you to walk off your temper, then come here and have a good sleep.'

He set her on the bed. She would have jumped up if he hadn't been so firmly by her with his hands on her waist. Should she try and hack that long shin so close to her bare foot? But no, the very thought of hurting him filled her eyes with tears. And when he kissed her eyes, each in turn, the tears spilt over.

'That's a bit how I felt——' he mopped them with a corner of the duvet '—when I went to your flat, and you weren't in it.'

'Good!' she told him on a giant hiccup. 'If I had been, I'd have put all the furniture against the door.'

'I've lots to tell you, so hold still and listen. Jamesina was born about two——'

'Jamesina?' Taffy echoed, distracted in spite of her misery. 'You're surely not going to call the poor little thing that?'

'And when we went in to make a fuss of them both, the way you've got to,' he went on with rebuking clam, 'damned if Claudia didn't insist I ring Alaska. At once. And keep ringing till I got through.'

'Alaska? Not Arizona, where the papers said she'd gone?' Taffy queried, intrigued in spite of herself. 'By the way, who gave them that story?'

'I did. Indirectly, through her agent.'

'I might have known. Another example of your skill as a——'

'Don't say it!' He put a hand over her mouth, and kept it there this time in spite of all her struggles. 'So, Alaska it had to be. It took me an hour.' He paused, maddeningly relaxed now that he had her helpless and gagged. 'Then I drove my mother to the flat for what was left of the night.'

The iron and amber eyes met Taffy's with puzzling intensity, and he took his hand from her mouth as if he expected a comment. 'She's staying in town for a few days.'

'To visit her grandchild?'

'I expect she'll visit Claudia and Jamesina, but they're not relations. Not even, thank heaven——' his eyes rose in a thankfulness that could almost have been sincere '—through Nick.'

'Nick?' Taffy frowned. 'You surely didn't think *he* was the father of this baby?'

'I didn't know what to think. And Claudia wasn't saying.'

'But...it could be yours?' She stared at him, wavering at last in her certainty of his guilt. 'You've been lovers?'

'Never.' He shook his head slowly and emphatically, his eyes holding hers. 'Not even ten years ago, when we were at college together.'

'But...taking her to Federange...'

'Everybody looks after Claudia—don't you remember?'

His eyes sought her understanding, and, reluctantly, she had to give it. She knew vividly the hurt-child pathos of this famous woman, all the more striking because she should have been so hard and glossy and invincible. Only last night Taffy had found herself responding to it through all her own pain.

'My mother, too,' he went on. 'Once she got fond of
Claudia, everything had to be *my* fault.'

'And she wanted you married before the baby came.'
Scraps of yesterday's talk came back to her, with new
meaning. 'You said she drives a hard bargain—was that
it? That she'd look after Claudia on condition you
married her?'

'Idiot!' He lifted one of her wet curls, and let it fall.
'As if I'd ever agree to anything like that!'

'So you did all this for *friendship*?'

'Friends matter too, dormouse. We go back a long
way, Claudia and me. She couldn't travel, she needed
privacy...' He broke off with a superb shrug. 'I fixed
it the Monday after the *Scheuberfouer*.'

She recalled the long-drawn-out torture of that
Monday, the slow-fading hope that he would reappear
in her life. 'That's when I thought you'd dropped me.'

'Did you?' He smiled with the old, loving mockery.
'I think of it as the time you vowed to be a career
woman.'

He was laughing at her and she loved it, loved
him...but wait. She mustn't let him fool her again.
Maybe he really was a friend in a million, a man to have
on your side against all the world—or maybe he was still
only a clever liar.

'Why didn't you tell me all this, Paul?'

'You can ask me that?' He stared at her in astonishment. 'It wasn't mine to tell.'

'Not mine to tell.' How the phrase brought it back,
his refusal to give away anything Claudia wouldn't want
known, and the lesson she had learnt from it in her
dealings with Nick.

And that was another thing. 'How did you keep Nick
away?'

'Didn't have to,' Paul grinned. 'He'd already paid his duty visit to his *Grand-mère*. He went home soon after.'

'But if you suspected the baby might be his...'

'It was still Claudia's secret, not mine. Thank heaven that's settled at last,' he added with feeling.

'It is?' Taffy interrupted. 'Are you allowed to tell now?'

'I'd damn well better be, after the trouble it's got me into.' He yawned again. 'But even my mother accepts now that Jamesina's father is Jim Grady...'

'Jim Grady?' Taffy felt her mouth drop open. 'Who's he?'

'A red-haired mining engineer, I gather, in Alaska. Where, until two o'clock this morning, Claudia didn't fancy living...'

'So it was him you had to ring?'

'He's on his way. And I hope for Jamesina's sake that he refuses to have his daughter named after him.' Paul covered yet another yawn. 'Now, can we forget Claudia and her affairs? Come and help me get back to sleep...'

'No!' She resisted his efforts to draw her close. 'You still haven't told me the hard bargain your mother drove.'

'Oh, that.' His hands rested on the hem of her T-shirt. 'It was only something I meant to do anyway.'

'And it is?'

'To marry a nice girl, and settle down in Federange, and run the wine business.'

'A nice girl.' Taffy suddenly realised how cold she felt. 'And seeing it isn't going to be Claudia, has your mother someone else picked out? A childhood sweetheart, maybe?'

'How did you guess?' In the brilliant, river-wavering snow light, his eyes suddenly seemed all iron. 'One of our neighbours has a daughter——'

Taffy couldn't listen to any more. 'So this is the end for us anyway.'

'Have you gone out of your mind?' He laid a hand on her forehead. 'You don't feel feverish...do you honestly believe I'd let my mother tell me who to marry?'

'When you put it like that, no,' she admitted. 'But you'd always do what's sensible.'

'You think so?' And now the amber showed in his eyes, warm and rueful. 'You think any sensible person would have got into the mess I've been in these last five months?'

She couldn't help seeing what he meant. 'Maybe what you did was better than sensible,' she acknowledged in a low voice. 'But it's over. You can do what you want again.'

'Right. Which is why we're meeting my mother for tea at four.' He pulled at the hem of the damp T-shirt. 'If you're not in bed with pneumonia by then.'

She grabbed his hands, and stopped them raising the T-shirt past the point of no return. 'Why am I to meet your mother?'

'Isn't it obvious? I should have taken you to Federange months ago.' His hands, frustrated on the T-shirt, moved to her trousers. 'I couldn't, though, while Claudia was there...'

'Because of your mother having the wrong idea,' she finished for him, pulling up the zip he had lowered.

'Not only that, Claudia was very edgy and secretive. You know what pregnant women are like...'

'I don't.' Taffy took a deep breath. 'But I soon might.'

'What?' He glanced up at her with a startled frown. 'Oh. You mean yesterday.'

'Is that all you have to say?'

'Naturally I'd rather not. I want you to myself for a bit, before we start a family...ugh!' He had begun to gather her in his arms, but now held her away with his hands on her shoulders. 'Taffy Griffin, if you don't get those disgusting wet things off, I'll... I'll tear them off.'

He would, too. She knew it, and knew what he'd do after, and saw that he easily could. The sight sent a flush of heat through her skin which quite cancelled out the chill of the wet clothes, yet still she resisted.

'And if you do that,' she countered, 'I'll get some more snow, and this time...' She left a wicked, insinuating pause. 'I wonder where I'll put it this time?'

'You dare!' He grabbed her firmly by the waist. 'What's eating you now, anyway? I've said it'll be fine about the baby if there is one...'

'You've never once mentioned marriage, though, have you?'

'Yes, I have. I told you I'm marrying a nice girl...'

'Which rules me out. I'm not a nice girl,' she pointed out, only half joking. 'I'm a girl who jumped into bed with a man she'd only known for six hours.'

'Ah, but that was me,' he responded with serene confidence. 'You won't ever do it with anyone else.'

'Won't I?' She let her eyes travel the perfect length of him, the long legs and flat belly and wide shoulders, the rampant manhood she so loved. 'How will you stop me?'

'I think you know the answer to that. All the answers.'

He thrust an impatient hand inside the top of her trousers, and with one sharp tug sent the button flying. It rattled and rolled away over the floor, leaving the zip to slide slowly open.

'Now, do I have to get rid of the rest the same way?' he demanded. 'Or will you be sensible and take them off?'

'I'll take them off,' she assured him. 'But only when...' She looked down, aware of her own blush, aware of those hot hands on her chilled flesh, impatient to set it on fire as they so often had, so easily could. 'When you've said the words,' she finished with difficulty.

'Words? What words?'

'The words that'll make it so that I never...' She stopped as he slid the T-shirt up over her head. 'Ever do this with anyone else,' she finished as she emerged from it.

'What, like I'd break his neck?' He flung the T-shirt away, and pulled her to her feet so that he could bear down on her trousers. 'Honestly, Taffy!' Down went the trousers, and down, and down. 'What a way to talk to the man who's going to be your husband.'

'Is he, Paul?' Still she held away from him, though he had swung her up naked against his own naked chest. 'How do I know until he's asked me?'

'So that's it.' He laid her on the bed, and stretched splendidly alongside her. 'You want it done formally. All right, then.' He kissed one of her breasts, and then the other. 'Miss Davina Griffin, will you marry me?'

Welcome to Europe

LUXEMBOURG—'the green heart of Europe' and 'the Gibraltar of the North'

With its royal family, fairy-tale castles, beautiful landscape and its position at the very heart of Europe—bordered by Belgium, Germany and France—Luxembourg is possibly one of the most romantic lands in the world.

FAMOUS LANDMARKS...

For its size Luxembourg contains many famous and interesting landmarks. The road which enters the city from the east crosses the tongue of rock known as the **Bock**. In the city itself, visitors will be enchanted by the old quarter of **Pfaffenthal** with its many medieval buildings. The **Rue de la Loge** is a quaint street, under two yards wide in places, while the **Place-Guillaume** is filled with shops and a colourful market place. The **Marché aux Poissons** is another square, less romantically known, in translation, as 'Fish Market Square'. In a city which inspired the artist Turner to paint some spectacular views, the **Pescatore Museum** contains priceless works of art by Dutch and French painters.

181

The many nations which invaded Luxembourg in the past have left *their* landmarks too: the **Casemates** are twenty-three km of underground military passages, barracks and chambers hewn from the rock by the Austrians and Spanish. The occupying French left behind walkways, turrets and ramparts, above the ground. In a country which still boasts a royal family, one would, perhaps, expect to find a royal palace, but there is also the beautiful cathedral shrine to **Our Lady of Luxembourg**, and, in keeping with the fairy-tale feel of the country and city, the **Fort of The Three Acorns** and the **Malakoff Tower**. And, finally, in a land which contains a thousand bridges, the **Grande Duchesse Charlotte Bridge** soars 280 feet above the **River Alzette.**

THE ROMANTIC PAST...

Luxembourg had a chequered and troubled past—invaded and conquered by many other nations, it finally became Lutzelburg in 963, under Sigefroi, the youngest count of Ardennes.

Among the House of Luxembourg's most famous founders was John the Blind, who was led unseeingly into battle and death with the English. The victorious Black Prince adopted John's symbol of the three feathers and his motto '*Ich Dien*' ('I serve') which are still used by Britain's current Prince of Wales.

In 1867 a meeting of the European countries certified Luxembourg's freedom and, in 1868, the free state of the Duchy of Luxembourg was created.

Perhaps because of the many centuries of change,

Luxembourg's motto '*Mir wölle bleiwe wat mir sin*' ('We wish to remain as we are') is extremely appropriate. Modern visitors can see this motto in a round bay window in Fish Market Square.

The most romantic legend associated with Luxembourg must be that of Sigefroi and Melusine. Sigefroi was out riding through the countryside one day when he fell in love with a beautiful maiden sitting on a rock, combing her hair. They married, but Melusine insisted that she must be left alone on Saturday nights. Because he loved her, Sigefroi respected Melusine's wishes for many years, but then, his jealousy and suspicion fuelled by the whispers of his friends, Sigefroi began to fear the worst. One Saturday he spied upon Melusine and discovered her secret—she was bathing in her true form—she was a mermaid. Because Sigefroi had betrayed her trust, Melusine was turned immediately into a rock and there she remains. One day, it is said, a brave man will wake the sleeping Melusine and Luxembourg will be his for the taking.

THE ROMANTIC PRESENT—pastimes for lovers...

Luxembourg today is one of the homes of the European Parliament—the building can be seen in the **Kirchberg**—and an important centre for international banking. In spite of its place in the modern world, however, Luxembourg still retains its timeless charm...it is a city well suited to lovers walking hand in hand along the **Corniche**, or wandering through the many narrow streets and colourful market squares.

What could be more romantic than a boat trip along the evocative **River Moselle**? And surely a trip on the miniature train can only add to the fairy-tale atmosphere of this magical place?

As might be expected, Luxembourg abounds in romantic rituals—on **'Bread Sunday'** in Lent, for instance, the man gives the lady of his choice a gift of bread; on Easter Sunday, the lady, in turn, offers her man an egg; and, on Easter Monday, they exchange gifts of little earthenware birds.

Luxembourg is a land of music and parades. The **Place-d'Armes** rings to the sound of concerts throughout the summer and anyone who visits Luxembourg is almost bound to see a parade, accompanied by innumerable bands.

In **Glacis Square**, in late August or early September, visitors will be treated to the **Scheuberfouer/Schobermesse** or Shepherd's Market, established in 1340 by John the Blind. On Sunday, traditionally dressed shepherds parade with decorated sheep through the city, to the tune of the **Hammelsmarsch**. The event is celebrated with roundabouts and sideshows and the whole city takes on a festive air.

For **lovers of food**,. Luxembourg offers the tasty dish *Judd matt Gaardebounen* (smoked pork with broad beans). Dishes of fish or ham will be equally pleasing to the traveller, while those with a sweet tooth will find a visit to one of the many pastry shops rewarding. A *tarte au quetsch* (plum tart) or an *omelette soufflé au kirsch* could easily be shared with a loved one, though the visitor could be forgiven for keeping these treats a secret!

The local beers and wines, particularly **Moselle**, are excellent, and the local *kirsch* is guaranteed to give even the most unromantic nature a lift!

Finally, for those who wish to take home a souvenir of their visit to this charming land and city, look for *Taaken*, miniature versions of Luxembourg's traditional decorated cast-iron fire doors. Or examples of pottery—it is surely an extremely romantic gesture to take home one of the little earthenware birds to recall a romantic tradition from Luxembourg, a magical and romantic land.

DID YOU KNOW THAT:

*Luxembourg has its own **currency** and its own elected **government**
*Its most important **exports** are iron and steel
*Luxembourg's **roses** are valued for their hardiness as well as their beauty
*The Dutch **flag** is also the flag of Luxembourg
*French is the official **language** of Luxembourg, but German and Letzeburgesch are equally recognised, while the use of English is widespread
*"I love you" in Letzeburgesch is either: *'Ech hunn dech garen'* OR *'Ech sinn frou matt dir'*.

LOOK OUT FOR ONE TITLE EVERY MONTH IN OUR SERIES OF EUROPEAN ROMANCES:

HAUNTING ALLIANCE: Catherine George (Portugal)
Catherine hadn't dreamed she'd find Eduardo Barroso so attractive—so why did she want to deny their love?

THE BRUGES ENGAGEMENT: Madeleine Ker (Belgium)
Geraldine had no intention of getting involved with Jan Breydel—but he was *dangerously* attractive, and the fairy-tale atmosphere of Bruges was working its magic...

YESTERDAY'S AFFAIR: Sally Wentworth (United Kingdom)
Nick Vaux had told Olivia he loved her, but then he walked away. Now Olivia had the chance to make him face his promises of the past!

DIAMOND HEART: Susanne McCarthy (Netherlands)
Was rich and powerful Piet den Ouden really fooled by Charlie's tearaway image...or had he glimpsed the vulnerable girl looking for love underneath?

MASK OF DECEPTION: Sara Wood (Italy)
Why was Lucenzo Salviati so determined that Meredith leave Venice? Was it because of her family's secrets— or the intense attraction between them?

Next Month's Romances

Each month you can choose from a wide variety of romance with Mills & Boon. Below are the new titles to look out for next month, why not ask either Mills & Boon Reader Service or your Newsagent to reserve you a copy of the titles you want to buy — just tick the titles you would like and either post to Reader Service or take it to any Newsagent and ask them to order your books.

Please save me the following titles:	Please tick	√
RIDE THE STORM	Emma Darcy	
A DAUGHTER'S DILEMMA	Miranda Lee	
PRIVATE LIVES	Carole Mortimer	
THE WAYWARD WIFE	Sally Wentworth	
HAUNTING ALLIANCE	Catherine George	
RECKLESS CRUSADE	Patricia Wilson	
CRY WOLF	Amanda Carpenter	
LOVE IN TORMENT	Natalie Fox	
STRANGER PASSING BY	Lilian Peake	
PRINCE OF DARKNESS	Kate Proctor	
A BRIDE FOR THE TAKING	Sandra Marton	
JOY BRINGER	Lee Wilkinson	
A WOMAN'S LOVE	Grace Green	
DANGEROUS DOWRY	Catherine O'Connor	
WEB OF FATE	Helena Dawson	
A FAMILY AFFAIR	Charlotte Lamb	

If you would like to order these books in addition to your regular subscription from Mills & Boon Reader Service please send £1.70 per title to: Mills & Boon Reader Service, P.O. Box 236, Croydon, Surrey, CR9 3RU, quote your Subscriber No:.......................................
(If applicable) and complete the name and address details below. Alternatively, these books are available from many local Newsagents including W.H.Smith, J.Menzies, Martins and other paperback stockists from 6th November 1992.

Name:..

Address:...

....Post Code:...........................

To Retailer: If you would like to stock M&B books please contact your regular book/magazine wholesaler for details.

You may be mailed with offers from other reputable companies as a result of this application.
If you would rather not take advantage of these opportunities please tick box ☐

PRESENT
THE 50TH ROMANCE BY
JESSICA STEELE
'DESTINED TO MEET'

Popular Romance author Jessica Steele finds her inspiration by travelling extensively and researching her backgrounds. But she hates to leave her delightfully soppy Staffordshire Bull Terrier, Daisy, behind, and likes nothing better than to work in her study overlooking a beautiful Worcestershire valley, backed by a hill and a long stretch of trees – "an ideal spot for writing" she says.

You're sure to agree when you read her latest intriguing love story *'Destined to Meet'* – don't miss it!

Published: October 1992   Price: £1.70

WIN A TRIP TO ITALY

Three lucky readers and their partners will spend a romantic weekend in Italy next May. You'll stay in a popular hotel in the centre of Rome, perfectly situated to visit the famous sites by day and enjoy the food and wine of Italy by night. During the weekend we are holding our first International Reader Party, an exciting celebratory event where you can mingle with Mills & Boon fans from all over Europe and meet some of our top authors.

HOW TO ENTER

We'd like to know just how wonderfully romantic your partner is, and how much Mills & Boon means to you.

Firstly, answer the questions below and then fill in our tie-breaker sentence:

1. **Which is Rome's famous ancient ruin?**

   ❏ The Parthenon ❏ The Colosseum ❏ The Sphinx

2. **Who is the famous Italian opera singer?**

   ❏ Nana Mouskouri ❏ Julio Iglesias ❏ Luciano Pavarotti

3. **Which wine comes from Italy?**

   ❏ Frascati ❏ Liebfraumilch ❏ Bordeaux

Tie-Breaker: Well just how romantic is your man? Does he buy you chocolates, send you flowers, take you to romantic candlelit restaurants? Send us a recent snapshot of the two of you (passport size is fine), together with a caption which tells us in no more than 15 words what makes your romantic man so special you'd like to visit Rome with him as the weekend guests of Mills & Boon.

....

....

....

....

Mills & Boon

In order to find out more about how much Mills & Boon means to you, we'd like you to answer the following questions:

1. How long have you been reading Mills & Boon books?

❑ One year or less ❑ 2-5 years ❑ 6-10 years

❑ 10 years or more

2. Which series do you usually read?

❑ Mills & Boon Romances ❑ Medical Romances ❑ Best Seller

❑ Temptation ❑ Duet ❑ Masquerade

3. How often do you read them? ❑ 1 a month or less

❑ 2-4 a month ❑ 5-10 a month ❑ More than 10 a month

Please complete the details below and send your entry to: Mills & Boon Reader Service, FREEPOST, P.O. Box 236, Croydon, Surrey CR9 9EL, England.

Name: ....

Address: ....

.... Post Code: ....

Are you a Reader Service subscriber?

❑ No ❑ Yes my Subscriber No. is: ....

_____ RULES & CONDITIONS OF ENTRY _____

1. Only one entry per household.
2. Applicants must be 18 years old or over.
3. Employees of Mills & Boon Ltd., its retailers, wholesalers, agencies or families thereof are not eligible to enter.
4. The competition prize is as stated. No cash alternative will be given.
5. Proof of posting will not be accepted as proof of receipt.
6. The closing date for entries is 31st December 1992.
7. The three entrants with correct answers who offer tie-breaker sentences considered to be the most appropriate and original will be judged the winners.
8. Winners will be notified by post by 31st January 1993.
9. The weekend trip to Rome and the Reader Party will take place in May 1993.
10. It is a requirement of the competition that the winners attend the Reader Party and agree to feature in any publicity exercises.
11. If you would like your snapshot returned, please enclose a SAE and we'll return it after the closing date.
12. To obtain a list of the winning entries, send a SAE to the competition address after 28th February, 1993.

You may be mailed with offers from other reputable companies as a result of this application. Please tick the box if you would prefer not to receive such offers. ❑

BARBARY WHARF

W(((O)))RLDWIDE

BRAND NEW MINI SERIES

As you know there are six books in total. Why not reserve your copies and receive two each month from Mills & Boon Reader Service for only £2.99 each, postage and packing FREE, or enclose a cheque for £17.94 made payable to Mills & Boon to receive all six books at once. Either way you will not miss any of these exciting future titles.

To reserve your **BARBARY WHARF** series, simply complete the coupon below and return it to:-

Mills & Boon Reader Service, FREEPOST PO Box 236, Croydon, CR9 9EL.

MINI SERIES

- ✂

PLEASE TICK ONE BOX ONLY:

☐ **YES!** Please reserve me a subscription to the **BARBARY WHARF** mini series. I understand that you will send me two books each month and invoice me for £5.98.　EPBW1

☐ **YES!** Please send me all six books in the **BARBARY WHARF** mini series. I enclose a cheque for £17.94. Postage and packing free.　EPBW2

Ms/Mrs/Miss/Mr _____

Address _____

_____

_____ Postcode _____

Signature _____

Are you a Reader Service Subscriber　Yes ☐　No ☐

Subscription No. _____